David Burnell was born and
at Cambridge, taught the sub
career applying the subject to management problems in the Health
Service, coal mining and latterly the water industry. On "retiring"
he completed a PhD at Lancaster on the deeper meaning of data
from London's water meters.

He and his wife live in Berkshire but own a small holiday cottage
in North Cornwall. They have four grown-up children.

Pebbles on the shore

Full-length stories by David Burnell

Doom Watch: *"Cornwall and its richly storied coast has a new writer to celebrate in David Burnell. His crafty plotting and engaging characters are sure to please crime fiction fans." Peter Lovesey*

Slate Expectations: *"combines an interesting view of an often overlooked side of Cornish history with an engaging pair of sleuths who follow the trail from past misdeeds to present murder." Carola Dunn*

"This book has an original atmospheric setting, which is sure to put Delabole on the map. A many-stranded story keeps the reader guessing, with intriguing local history colouring events up to the present day." Rebecca Tope

Looe's Connections: *"History, legend, and myth mixed with a modern technical conundrum make this an intriguing mystery." Carola Dunn*

"A super holiday read set in a super holiday location!" Judith Cutler

Peter Lovesey is a winner of the CWA Cartier Diamond Dagger.

Carola Dunn authors the Daisy Dalrymple and Cornish mysteries.

Rebecca Tope writes the Cotswold and West Country Mysteries.

Judith Cutler is author of several crime series, most recently featuring Detective Superintendant Fran Harman

PEBBLES ON THE SHORE

David Burnell

Pebbles on the shore

First published August 2015.

Photographs taken by David Burnell and Chris Scruby.

ISBN-13: 978-1515184683
ISBN-10: 1515184684

Pebble-patterns on a shore in the Scilly Isles.

The front cover shows the Cornish coast at
Crackington Haven

FORWARD

We've all had the experience of walking across a pebble-strewn shore. One of the surprising things is the variety of shapes and the mixture of size, colour and texture in the pebbles that we step over. Some pebbles are beautiful, round and smooth, while others are odd-shaped or rough. The pattern may seem random but if we look carefully and use our imagination we can sometimes see a semblance of order.

The stories in this book are like that – murky or quirky. Some are crime stories, often involving murder. As in real life there are a variety of outcomes. Others are salutary tales from everyday life. A few are primarily comic. If you haven't been prompted to laugh by the time you've read them all then I have failed. One or two, less funny, are concerned with espionage.

Some stories form a mini-series - best read in the order they appear. But I've deliberately mixed up the categories, like pebbles on the shore.

Most stories are set in the present day but one or two deal with life in a previous century. They happen in a variety of locations, most in the UK. In the majority of cases the cast is fully human.

My main output as a writer are the Cornish Conundrums, full-length crime stories, set around Cornwall. None of these stories overlap with the Conundrums; you don't need to read one before the other. Occasional picture notes link the two species.

Assembling a collection of short stories can't be rushed. These have arisen from Writers' Circle challenges over the last three years. But drawing them together has been a chance to give them an extra polish.

I will be delighted if you enjoy the reading as much as I've enjoyed the writing. But don't expect every aspect of every story to be fully resolved.

David Burnell   Website: davidburnell.info
August 2015

Another pebbly shore at Millmouth, near Hartland Point.

CONTENTS

Pebbles on the shore

1.   THATCHED AND DESPATCHED

'I'm John Dennis, thatcher, specialist in top level reconstruction.'

It was an odd introduction but the rustic-looking man waited, looking hopeful rather than self-deluded, at the vicarage door. Gove-like grammar was unlikely to be high on his skill set.

'Good morning, Mr Thatcher, how can I help you?' It had crossed the Vicar's mind to respond that he was Sir Geoffrey Howe but right now he was too busy for political role-play.

'No, no, sir. You misunderstand.' The man spoke with a delightful Norfolk burr. 'I'm a thatcher - from Thetford, near Norwich. My name is John Dennis. Are you not expecting me?'

Peering behind the flamboyant figure, the Vicar could see a giant trailer of reed, parked outside his gate. Dimly he recalled overhearing some conversation in the Speckled Hen a month or two back, to the effect that two or three of the villagers planned to make good use of the fine weather to refurbish their bedraggled thatched roofs – and that it would be cheaper to do the jobs all at the same time. This hairy character, looking like an extract from a latter-day Dickens novel, must be the outcome.

'It's probably my housekeeper you need to talk to.' The Vicar turned and called down the hall. 'Matilda. There's someone here I think may be for you.'

A harassed-looking woman bustled up the passage and took in the scene at a glance. 'Ah, better late than never, I suppose. We wuzz expecting you yesterday.'

John Dennis was about to start on some excuse but Matilda

1

silenced him with a cursory wave and turned to the Vicar.

'Can I be off now, sir? Everything's tidy, I think. This gentleman needs to be shown which roofs he's to work on. After all, time is money with his profession.' It was obvious that in Matilda's mind the same economic discipline did not apply to the Vicar.

She and the thatcher wandered off down the path and the Vicar returned to his half-finished sermon. Pressure to bring an ill man to Jesus had caused a roof to be dismantled rather than rebuilt. He wondered if he could recast the event from the viewpoint of the local roof man.

The Vicar had a sprawling country parish. Once a month he would take a week over a grand tour, staying a night in each outlying village. The evening after his return, on his usual stroll, the Vicar came across John Dennis, sitting on his own outside the Speckled Hen. If he could only remember the bloke's name it was a chance to make amends.

'Ah, Mr . . . Dennis, what'll you have?'

'Oh, thank 'ee. Mine's a Marston's Special.'

Glancing more carefully, the Vicar noted the thatcher already had a nearly-full glass in front of him - but the offer had now been made. A few minutes later two pints arrived at the table.

'I'm sorry, I was a bit confused when we met last week,' the Vicar began. 'I'd forgotten all about the planned thatching work. How's it going?'

'It's early days, Vicar. Your housekeeper got me three jobs to do in the village but I'm onto the second cottage now – Mrs Brice's. I managed to get all the old thatch off today so I'll be able to start laying down the new reed tomorrow morning.'

'You're hoping it won't rain tonight, then?' the Vicar smiled. 'Or at least, Mrs Brice is.'

'I'm not worried. It's going to be fine for another three days - great for thatchers everywhere. I've worked fourteen hours today -

it'll be the same tomorrow and Thursday.'

Impressive. Despite appearances Dennis was hard working – was there a sermon illustration here somewhere?

'So where are you staying?'

'Oh, I just sleeps in my trailer - up on the reeds. As well as saving money it gives me some security.' He smiled. 'I'm hoping for a fine night too.'

'Hm. It's a pity your contract didn't cover accommodation. There's bound to be someone here who could put you up for a couple of weeks – Mrs Brice, for example.'

Dennis looked at him with alarm. 'I wouldn't fancy that. She holds séances in the afternoons, so goodness knows what she does at night. I don't think she realised how much I could hear when I was working up on her roof. Some of those spells seemed pretty threatening.'

The thatcher sipped his drink and laughed. 'In fact, you featured in one of them.' He gave the Vicar's head a rapid survey. 'But you've not gone bald - so it doesn't seem to have worked.'

The Vicar had not expected the conversation to move this way. He'd had reservations about Mrs Brice before but this was hard evidence: he would need to take action of some sort, or at least consult the Bishop. But that was for later. 'You must hear a lot while you're up on the roof?'

'And see plenty as well – especially when I've got the old reeds off but the new ones aren't yet laid. It's . . . well, it's almost like a physical confession.'

And more reliable, thought the Vicar. Most confessions he'd heard had been watered down for his consumption. Better make the most of the moment.

'So what else can you tell me about life in the village?'

'The cottage I worked on first – that's Mr Breedon's – did you know he runs a twice-weekly gambling session?'

'Good heavens, I did not. Is that cards or horses?'

3

'You're behind the times, Vicar. Nowadays it's all via the internet. Mostly wild fights in far-flung places. But Breedon keeps his punters on a tight rein. And supplies them with a strong punch, which I reckons is far from legal. I've seen him distil it himself in his back room. I guess, since there's no tax, he makes plenty on it.'

'Well, what a surprise. He's a solicitor, you know.'

'Should know better, then. But the establishment looks after its own. He won't be caught, will he?'

The Vicar had expected to be the provider of information - this was all the wrong way round. John Dennis had learned more about the failings of the village in a week than he had discovered in a decade.

It was some time before he returned to the vicarage for what turned out to be a disturbed night's sleep.

It was three nights later, as the heat wave ended, that the fire began. The weather had been fine for almost a month, the grass of the village green was a dismal yellow and local vegetation was as dry as a bone. No-one ever knew how the blaze started. One suggestion was that an abandoned garden bonfire or barbeque had provided an airborne spark, which flourished on the gentle evening breeze.

By midnight there was no-one walking around the village, though there were plenty of windows open. So for a long time there was no-one in a position to observe the effect of the spark on the trailer-load of dry reed.

Thatchers often claim that the fire risk from a thatched roof is small; treated reeds should smoulder rather than blaze. But the reeds in John Dennis's trailer were not yet treated and they too had dried in the fine weather. They were far from non-flammable, though they burnt only slowly. But the high walls of the trailer meant that the fire inside was not seen for many hours; and the fire brigade were not called until early next morning.

4

By breakfast, as villagers emerged from their cottages, the brigade had taken remedial action and the trailer was a buckled mass of metal, containing a hot, steaming concoction of dark, soggy ashes.

'Good job there was no one inside,' observed the Fire Officer. 'And thank heavens the trailer was parked well away from other buildings.'

'I hope John Dennis had proper insurance,' murmured one of the villagers. 'Where is he, anyway?' It was a good question.

'When it cools it might just be worth checking that there was no-one inside,' one of the villagers advised the Fire Officer a few minutes later. 'Our visiting thatcher seems to have disappeared.'

Two hours later their worst fears were confirmed. There was indeed a skeleton amidst all the burnt out reeds. Soon after that Inspector Johnson arrived.

The most likely – the most convenient - scenario was a tragic accident. Everyone in the village would be happy with that, not least the owners of the newly-thatched cottages with no-one to demand payment for their new roofs. John Dennis had cut one corner too many by sleeping in his trailer and had just been very unlucky. But that left Johnson with a few loose ends.

Most significantly, the fire brigade could not guarantee that the fire was an accident. There were a few odd marks inside the trailer, they said, that could possibly have resulted from ignited petrol.

There was no good reason to suspect suicide. Dennis's current project, Johnson learned, was with Mrs Brice. When the policeman interviewed her she spoke warmly of the roofer's enthusiasm. And surely not even the most melancholic would choose the agony of a slow roasting.

The policeman also had words with Mr Breedon. He sensed something was being left unsaid but he wasn't good enough at mind-reading to work out what.

5

Johnson struggled to find Dennis's base address so he could alert the next of kin. All the man's paperwork had been lost in the fire and none of the new-thatch owners had a copy. They'd left the choice of thatcher to Matilda Henderson, convenor of the Women's Institute, but she seemed to have disappeared, along with the Vicar.

In these camera-mad days the Inspector would have expected someone to take a photo, but though he could find several pictures of the village's new roofs, all glinting in the sun, none were of the John Dennis who'd created them. It was unthinkable to display the man's heat-engulfed skull on television, even on Crime Watch. But what was the alternative? His boss ruled out spending a fortune, asking a forensic scientist to rebuild the head from the cooked remains plus recent village memories.

Whatever else, it had been a spectacular incident. Johnson could only hope the publicity would hit the man's home town. If it did turn into a murder case he would need to know as much as possible about the victim and who might conceivably have reason to kill him.

Oddly, though, no-one ever came forward with a back-story which matched both the name and the profession.

On the same morning as the trailer fire, a small car drove onto the channel ferry with a middle-aged couple on board. Embarkation was easy: no delays at Customs. Six hours later the pair disembarked at Cherbourg and continued steadily on to their newly rented cottage in the Dordogne.

Matilda gave a great sigh of relief. Soon she could start the process of reinventing herself as a French citizen. Her days of vicarage housekeeping were over.

It did not take her companion long to start another fire, this one in the garden. Then Matilda brought out the suitcase of papers associated with her old life and threw them, one by one, into the flames.

John Dennis, thatcher, also had papers to burn. His identity had lasted for less than a fortnight and would never be seen again. He had taken great care during his time as a thatcher to make sure he was never photographed; and once he'd removed the false hair and beard he'd worn for the fortnight he was unrecognisable any-way. The beard wouldn't be needed for thatching in France.

'Even better than we'd hoped,' he remarked, as they settled down to a quiet evening meal. 'I got the Vicar feeling so guilty he insisted on swapping places with me for the crucial night - we didn't even have to drag him in to the trailer. He was a great stand-in: with luck no-one will ever notice the exchange.'

2. RURAL RE-ENACTMENT

'Inspector Johnson?'

As the policeman seized the phone, he struggled to remember how to address a Bishop. 'Yes, Your Grace,' he guessed. 'How can I help?'

'I got your name from the newspapers, Inspector. They said you were the one investigating that dreadful fire at Stowell?'

'That's right, sir. A very sad case. Their visiting thatcher was burnt to death in his own truck.'

'Good, good.' Obviously the thatcher was not the focus of his concern.

'I wondered if, while you were there, you had any contact with the Vicar of Stowell – Kevin Marshall? The thing is, he was due to lead a session at our Retreat Centre this morning and he hasn't shown up. Or sent an apology. I've just rung his vicarage: he's not there either. That's not like him at all.'

'I'm afraid I never met the Reverend Marshall, sir. He wasn't around at the time of the fire. The locals thought he'd gone on holiday. He was a bit absent-minded, they said, would go off from time to time for a few days. He was into landscape painting. Maybe . . . maybe he's lost track of time?'

'But the fire was three weeks ago, Inspector. I've checked with colleagues: no-one's heard a word. That's why I'd like to report him missing. I can supply a photograph – though I'm afraid it's not very up-to-date. What else do you need?'

8

Inspector Johnson was not convinced he'd got the whole story at Stowell but his boss had hastened him on to "real crime". Not only was the Vicar absent, he recalled, but his housekeeper had gone as well. That was equally bizarre: surely the two wouldn't have gone off together?

He pored over Marshall's personnel file which the Bishop had sent over by courier. It was marked "Highly Confidential". As the policeman read, his concerns started to grow.

The Vicar had had an unusual past. He'd trained as a solicitor but something must have gone wrong. Fifteen years ago he'd ended up in Ford Open Prison, serving time for fraud. There, it seemed, he had seen the light through an Alpha Course, put on by the Prison Chaplain. After prison he'd become very active in a town-centre church in Salisbury.

Four years on, Marshall had felt called to ordination, been accepted and spent three years at Theological College. Then he'd served as Curate in a Dorset village, before taking the post at Stowell. He'd been there for three years, nothing untoward was recorded: he was well regarded in church circles.

Johnson mused over the record. Not many priests had criminal records but he supposed that, if the church really believed in fresh starts, they had to be willing to accept a late convert. The Apostle Paul, he recalled, had rather a chequered past.

But even if he was now "as white as driven snow", might such a record leave a man open to blackmail?

The policeman let his mind wander. The trouble was, he knew so little about the victim. Could the mysterious thatcher - origin unknown - have discovered the Vicar's background and come to the village to apply pressure? The Vicar certainly would not want the news of his former life to be common knowledge: it would hardly enhance his ministry. So would that in turn have provided a real motive for the thatcher to be hastened on his way?

For the first time the Inspector allowed himself to consider the possibility that the Vicar's absence was linked in some way to the unexplained blaze. It was a wild idea; but the alternative - that the Vicar had gone away at exactly the same time as the fire - was peculiar as well.

Johnson consulted his notes. Yes, that was right. One of the villagers, Mrs Brice, had told him, 'The one who invited the thatcher to the village was Matilda. She's the woman that does the Vicar's cleaning.'

That was the link between the two men: Matilda knew them both. So in this wild scenario, was Matilda the one who had told the thatcher about the Vicar's former life? Had she learned something, say, while cleaning in the vicarage – something she'd passed on to the luckless thatcher?

Johnson studied the file again.

Marshall had never been married. Was there anything special about his relation to Matilda? Mrs Brice had told him, 'She's been his housekeeper for the last two years.'

Maybe, to help the Bishop, he needed to know more about how these two had met?

The policeman ploughed back through the file, looking for possible points of contact between Marshall and Matilda. He was about to give up when he came across a detail from Marshall's years after prison: the former inmate had taken up prison visiting. The Personnel Officer cited it as 'clear evidence of a change of lifestyle.' Good: prison visiting was a fine vocation.

But Johnson knew about prisons; and noticed that the prison where Marshall had put most of his efforts was a women's prison on the edge of Salisbury.

What if Matilda was a former prisoner there that Marshall had befriended - and later offered a job, once he found he needed a housekeeper?

As he thought around the idea, it made some sort of sense. Marshall had been thoroughly rehabilitated; in his new-found enthusiasm he might well want to extend the process to others. A housekeeping job in the middle of nowhere was as safe from temptation as anywhere.

But in that case, might Matilda know as much about the Vicar's past as he knew about hers?

This was pure speculation – but hard not to pursue. Johnson wondered what crime Matilda might have committed to land up in jail. A horrible thought came to him: had she been an arsonist?

Just a minute – he was a policeman, he didn't need to guess. What years had Marshall been prison visiting in Salisbury? He checked; then started tapping into the law enforcement grapevine.

An hour later, the policeman sat back, a smile on his face. He had had to pull a few strings but had finally got through to the governor of Salisbury Women's prison; and hence to the prison records for the years in question.

'Were there any prisoners at that time called Matilda?'

There was a pause. 'Just one: Matilda Hendrick.'

'What can you tell me about her?'

'She was about thirty; in for heavy-duty shop-lifting.'

Someone like that would certainly be helped by a move to the country. A few minutes later Johnson had been sent a photograph of Matilda, taken ten years ago. All he needed now was a trip to Stowell, to see if any residents there could recognise her.

A week later the Inspector started a fortnight's leave. He'd hoped to take the time as part of his job but his boss had no sympathy with his ideas. 'You've not got a shred of evidence of wrongdoing. Old prison records don't prove anything.'

Johnson could do what he liked, though, in his own time.

In the intervening days Mrs Brice had confirmed that Matilda Hendrick was the woman known in Stowell as Matilda Henderson, the Vicar's housekeeper. She'd also given him the registration number of the Vicar's car, an aged green Citroën, which was no longer at the vicarage.

Most crucial of all, Johnson had obtained the telephone records for the vicarage; and discovered a call made, just before the fire, to a Channel Ferry operating out of Portsmouth; and another to the owner of a holiday cottage in Sainte Alvère, in the Dordogne.

That sounded just the sort of place to take a holiday of his own.

It was mid-afternoon, three days later that the Inspector got out of a bus in Sainte Alvère, found a pension and booked in for a couple of days. Then he set out on foot for the cottage where the Vicar - or perhaps his housekeeper? - had been in touch a few weeks earlier.

It was another thatched cottage, with an overgrown garden. As he walked slowly up the drive, Johnson spotted a green car half-hidden in the bushes. Its number showed it belonged to the Vicar of Stowell. Relief – hard evidence at last that he was on the trail.

The policeman took a moment to order his thoughts then hammered at the door.

After a short delay a man came to answer. He didn't look much like the picture of the trainee vicar from the Bishop's file - but it could have been. This man was sun-tanned and clean-shaven whereas Mrs Brice had said the Vicar had had a beard: but that was easy to alter. The forthcoming dialogue would reveal all.

'Bonjour, monsieur.' The policeman was out of uniform but still carried the demeanour of authority.

The man looked uncomfortable. 'Bonjour,' he replied.

'Vous êtes anglais?'

'I'm as English as you are. What d'you want?'

It was time for the crunch question. 'Are you the Reverend Kevin Marshall?'

The man took stock. 'How do you know? I've come to France for a break – to get away from Stowell. Who are you, anyway?'

'My name is Johnson. Back in the UK I'm a policeman but I'm here in France on holiday. Could I come in for a few minutes?'

For two Englishmen, meeting abroad, there was no good reason to refuse. 'Please, come in. We'll sit in the conservatory. Would you like a glass of wine?'

Johnson followed the man through the cottage and out through the French window. There were several garden chairs around a cane table. He took one facing the lawn.

His host came out a moment later, carrying two glasses of red wine. 'Help yourself.' As he spoke, he picked up one himself and took a sip. 'Cheers. Now, what did you want to talk about? '

'Cheers,' responded the policeman. 'You left Stowell recently, Mr Marshall. Was that before or straight after the fire?'

'What fire?' The host looked bemused.

'You remember John Dennis, the thatcher? Well, the reed on his lorry caught fire: it was a massive blaze. Unfortunately the poor bloke was sleeping in the lorry at the time. He was reduced to a skeleton. I was the policeman called. Both you and Matilda had gone away. One reason for coming here is to check you are alright. And Matilda – am I right that she's here too?'

The host seemed to have some difficulty framing his reply.

The policeman picked up his glass again and had another gulp. Whatever else you might say about the French, they certainly produced top-class wine. This was delicious. He had a few more sips.

13

There was a noise behind and a woman appeared. It was Matilda. He recognised her from the photo which Mrs Brice had lent him.

Johnson stood to shake her hand. 'Mrs Henderson. My name is Johnson. I'm here about the fire in Stowell. I'm afraid it did for the thatcher.' He watched her carefully as he spoke. Was this new information? It was hard to tell.

The host was also looking hard at the woman. 'Mr Johnson is a policeman, Matilda. We must have left Stowell just before a fire. That poor thatcher – we should have offered him shelter, you know.'

Johnson had many questions but found it hard to concentrate. He had another drink. The wine was certainly very strong. Good job he hadn't driven here. It made him feel very sleepy. . . very sleepy indeed.

'We'll need to offer Mr Johnson a bed as well,' laughed Matilda. As she spoke the policeman slumped forward, unconscious.

'How long before he wakes up, John?'

The stand-in Vicar shrugged. 'A couple of hours. Check his pockets are empty then we'll get him into the car. They're bound to find him eventually, but we don't want that to be anywhere near here. Good job I'd doctored the wine beforehand. We're still ahead of the game, Matilda – let's keep it that way.'

3.   TABLES TURNED AT TOLPUDDLE

'Numpty!' I yelled.

Morag and I came round a bend then screeched to a halt, no more than a foot from a furniture van which was blocking the entire road. It was hard to be sure in the heavy rain, but its scowling driver looked to be no fun to argue with. He was in a hurry and, apparently, had no reverse gear.

My slow retreat, round the bend then into a muddy field, would have been easier without Morag's advice (why couldn't she tell left from right?) and without the feeling that the furniture van was hustling us every inch of the way. By the time he'd got past us I'd had enough and would cheerfully have followed him back to civilisation. But Morag still wanted to bag her trophy house.

It was the last day of our soggiest autumn holiday for years. Morag had developed a passion for Tolpuddle Manor: 'Hamish, it's their last day open this year,' she pleaded, 'at least we'll stay dry.' I would have preferred to set off back to Galloway and get away from the so-called Dorset desert.

Eventually we reached the Manor, a sprawling, half-timbered establishment with a thatched roof. Morag claimed it looked old and distinguished. I just thought it needed new paint.

'It's our last day,' the receptionist told us with an excited smile. 'Make the most of it: you may not see it again.'

It was ambiguous advice. 'Sounds dire,' I muttered to Morag, as we headed for the main hall, 'maybe the woodworm's finally taken over.'

But even I had to admit the main hall was splendidly antique -

15

although the tables around the panelled sides looked rather modern. There were various medieval games laid out; two children were engrossed in nine-man Morris, while two more were having a whale of a time thrashing a top across the wooden floor. A stern Elizabethan nobleman – a previous owner? - looked down from the picture over the fireplace with disapproval.

Why should the kids have all the fun? 'Do you reckon that suit of armour is for visitors to try?' I asked Morag.

'You'd never fit inside it,' she retorted.

'But don't you think the helmet would suit you?' I'd noticed a catch on the visor that could be fastened by a padlock. A period of conjugal silence would sooth our journey back to Scotland.

The manor had had an irregular history – or maybe we were going through it in the wrong order. Whatever the reason, the rooms moved backwards and forwards in time like episodes from Dr Who. According to the guidebook, we were in a Tudor dining room one minute, a Victorian bedroom the next, then a Georgian bathroom. The top floor was blocked off: maybe, I thought, that held the future?

But whatever the period, the wall-coverings looked more distinctive than the furniture.

Two hours later we'd completed the tour and were gasping for coffee; or something stronger in my case. Morag spotted a sign advertising "The Barn Cafe" out of the rear door and we headed for it.

It was a substantial building, away from the Manor; but today, the last day of the season, there were not many customers. Morag chose a table well away from the draughty door. As she studied the menu, I picked up a flyer.

'Morag, this must be some sort of joke. It says these tables and chairs are for sale.'

My spouse was deliberating whether I was to be allowed some cake; she took a moment to reply. 'Huh. But does it tell you the price they're after? They look very elaborate, mind – more stylish than the ones we saw in the Manor.'

'It says "Ask at the serving desk for details." There'd be no harm in asking.'

I should explain, by the way, that we did not believe in buying new furniture. The gifts given at our wedding, thirty years ago, would surely see us out. But our dining table in Galloway was the worse for wear; and several of the chairs now had wobbly backs. It was a hospitality challenge to make sure any guest was given a chair that could take their weight.

So, as I went up to order, I asked the kitchen manager – Sylvia, her name-tag said - what sort of prices they had in mind.

'You look shocked,' observed Morag as I returned.

'Morag, I can't believe this, but lady behind the counter says she wants just £5 per chair and £30 per table: in cash. No paper-work. She called it an "end-of-season sale".'

'Maybe this is our lucky day. It was bound to happen eventually - we'll buy some Lottery Tickets on the way home. So how many of these chairs do you reckon we could get into our Galaxy?'

As we drank our coffee, what had begun as a joke gradually became a reality. There was no doubt the solid oak table and the chairs we were sitting on were much better than anything we had at home.

'Logistics is no problem,' I remarked. 'Galaxies without their rear seats are capacious.'

Morag started to enthuse. 'We could get this table in upside down; then four chairs on top. That's all we need. We could never buy all that – even in a sale - for less than £50.'

Half an hour later a smiling Sylvia helped us reverse our Galaxy into the back yard; then to carry our newly-acquired furniture out to the car.

'I think she's done this before,' I told Morag, as we drove off.

'Now are you glad we came?'

17

'OK. This is the best value-for-money country house we've ever visited,' I admitted, as we drove carefully back to our holiday cottage. Mercifully, apart from ourselves, there were no more furniture vans on the road.

Several months later the new furniture was proving a great success in Galloway. We had moved on from a semi-reclusive existence, almost embarrassed to invite neighbours in, to being the social hub of the district. Telling guests that they were sitting on genuinely historic chairs was a good conversation starter.

'Where did you say this house was?' asked one of the guests, Mary McDonald, as the story was retold for the fourth time. It turned out that the McDonalds, too, had been on holiday in Dorset; but a fortnight after us.

'It's called Tolpuddle Manor; near Dorchester.'

'What a coincidence,' said Mr McDonald. 'We wanted to visit there, but we couldn't.'

'No, you wouldn't. We went on the last day of the season,' replied my wife. 'That's why they were selling stuff off.'

'Och no, Morag, that wasn't what stopped us at all. It was more fundamental than that. Surely you knew that the place caught fire? That happened just before we'd hoped to visit.'

Both of us were shocked. 'How dreadful,' said Morag. 'The Manor was a delight to walk round – quirkily historic. Was it badly damaged?'

'The main house was completely destroyed,' said Mr McDonald.

'There was no-one living there,' added his wife, 'once the season was over: no-one stayed over the winter. And as I'm sure you found, it's a remote place. I guess that meant it took a while before the alarm was given.'

Her husband took up the tale. 'All the fire brigade could do, when it eventually got there, was to preserve the barn behind the main house. And that was hardly a historic building.'

18

'It was actually the barn where these chairs came from,' I said. 'Mind you, Morag and I thought they looked more historic than the furniture in the Manor.'

'Almost as if someone had swapped them beforehand,' laughed Mary McDonald.

A light-hearted comment. But we remembered it later, when our guests had departed.

'The owners would only do something like that if they planned a massive insurance fraud,' I commented. 'They'd hope to claim huge amounts for the valuable furniture in the Manor, when in fact they'd just lost the dross used in the barn.'

There was a pause as we both considered possible scenarios.

'But do you remember, Hamish — that furniture van we nearly rammed on the way. That narrow road only went as far as Tolpuddle. What on earth was that doing? Was it taking other valuables out of the way?'

'But . . . all of that would only make sense if the owners knew beforehand there was going to be a fire.'

A pause, while each of our imaginations leapt forward.

'Yes... so you think they must also have arranged to start the fire at the house - as well as removing the most valuable items.'

'I suppose if you're really determined,' I mused, 'starting a fire at an old property in the back of beyond is not that difficult. After all, no-one was staying there, so there was no watchman - and no-one to get hurt.'

This was absurd. It was Dorset Dynasties we were talking about.

'But surely they wouldn't do that?'

'Depends on how financially desperate the owners were.'

We thought back to our visit. How prosperous did the Manor appear? I remembered the lack of paint; and the blocked-off floor.

'I don't know how many visitors they normally get at the end of the season,' I mused. 'It was the school half-term holiday. But it wasn't busy; maybe trade was down due to a lousy autumn?'

'Hey - do you remember that odd comment from the ticket woman?' asked Morag. 'Something about "our last chance to see the house".'

As we mused a fire-insurance conspiracy still seemed unlikely; but by no means impossible. Then I had a further thought.

'But if the owners did swap the best furniture in the Manor with the tables and chairs in the cafe, why on earth would the kitchen staff sell it on to visitors?'

There was a longer pause. Morag was the first to speak.

'Could that have been a separate scam? Perhaps . . . perhaps the kitchen staff saw what was going on and guessed what would happen next.'

'Then it would dawn on them that they would all lose their jobs once Tolpuddle Manor was destroyed.'

'Maybe that was their revenge? Sell on the best furniture while it was in the barn, and make a small bonus. No-one would notice in all the confusion.'

'So what do you think we should do about it?' I asked.

For an hour Morag and I sat across the table, wrestling with the few solid facts in our possession - and the many possible implications.

Finally I gave judgement. 'The truth is, we've no hard evidence that anything is wrong at all. We've got our chunk of country house furniture – and we paid for it – the asking price. Why should we do anything?'

'At least,' said Morag, tapping the table, 'some bits of Tolpuddle Manor weren't burnt in the fire. Let the folk of Galloway come and enjoy them.'

The National Trust's beautifully maintained Trerice House near Newquay. It's absolutely nothing like the fictional Tolpuddle Manor - but we do dine on chairs bought from their end-of-season sale.

4.   A TANGLE OF ACCIDENTS

It all started with an innocent tangle.

Hilary and Mark were washing their car together outside their rented holiday cottage at the end of a glorious summer holiday. They didn't normally bother with such refinements but the seagulls had made so much mess on their car – which had been parked every night on the jetty - that they feared the roof might corrode away unless swift action was taken.

All they had to work with was the bucket they'd found under the sink – plus the outdoor tap which the cottage owners had fitted for watering the garden. The Golf was parked on the road outside, the sun continued to shine; what could possibly go wrong?

The couple sponged away on either side of the car and it was Hilary's turn to have the bucket.

'Watch out, dear,' she called.

Mark stood back as a small amount of soapy water was thrown over the car roof.

Trivial. He moved forward again – just as the rest of the bucket followed to give a more significant dowsing. A small fraction caught the car but the bulk went on to the partner, leaving him covered from head to foot with cold water and soapy bubbles.

'Idiot,' he fumed. He wasn't referring to himself.

Hilary guessed what must have happened. She came round to his side of the car and creased up with laughter as she saw his bedraggled state.

'Mark, I'm so sorry,' she managed to splutter before further gales of laughter overtook her.

But Mark did not see the funny side. 'You will be,' he retorted, stepping forward to seize the bucket off her before turning to refill it. Why should he be the only one taking an impromptu cold shower?

Hilary saw how upset he was and put up her hands. 'No, no – please darling, these are my last clean clothes. It really was an accident. Honestly, I'm so dreadfully sorry.'

Reluctantly, Mark put down the bucket. Hilary sounded sincere and unusually contrite. He was still upset but could wait for his moment of retaliation.

His time came back home that evening as Hilary took her shower. One of the joys of being home, they'd agreed, was the recently-fitted power shower which gave them unlimited, piping hot water to bathe in. Or at least, would have done if it had been turned on.

Hilary had slipped off her spectacles so did not notice the line of buckets as she went into the bathroom, took off her remaining clothes and stepped into the shower.

Mark, who had quietly followed her into the bathroom, pulled the switch by the door to turn off the power. Then he seized the first bucket of cold water.

'This is what it felt like, dear,' he explained as he threw it over her.

Hilary gave a scream – she'd had her back to him and had been expecting hot water, not ten litres which was icy cold. The screams continued as the second, third and fourth buckets followed.

It took some time for her emotions to calm down. In the end she agreed that they were now all square and they managed to restore their relationship in a more intimate way.

It would all have ended there but for another calamity. Hilary was a teacher and used the rest of her summer holidays to redecorate the kitchen, putting fresh emulsion on the walls and re-glossing the door and windows. The many tins of paint were always kept in their garage.

At the end of a long, tiring day she was standing on tiptoe, easing the tin of gloss back onto its shelf over the garage door, when she heard the phone in the hall. Rushing back indoors, she picked it up just in time; and learned that her youngest niece had taken her first tiny steps.

'Hey, that's wonderful. Such a clever little girl. She gets it from her Auntie, you know.'

The sisters were still cooing happily over the event, half an hour later, when she heard a crash from the garage, followed by a howl of rage. 'Sorry, I'd better go.'

Afterwards Hilary could never explain exactly how it had happened. She suspected that Mark had come home in a bad mood and, as a result, opened the garage door with less than his usual care. Whatever the cause, the result had been to knock the delicately balanced gloss paint from its insecure location on the shelf.

And she was almost certain that she had, earlier, put its lid on properly. But she'd been painting all day, using lots of tins, and perhaps she had become careless – or tired - towards the end.

Whatever the cause, the effect was spectacular. The white gloss was now no longer in the tin but spread over the trousers of Mark's only business suit. And he was hopping round the garage like a luminescent ghost – but making far from ghost-like complaints at a decidedly non-ghostly volume.

To say he was upset did not do the situation justice - like observing that the Palestinians disagreed with the Israelis or that Ian Paisley was not best pals with Gerry Adams. The gist of his diatribe was that Hilary was "toast" – or would have been, had not the allegorical bread been reduced in its turn into carbon and ashes.

In vain did his partner apologise, grovel and plead for forgiveness. She agreed that he would need to buy a new suit from their joint account and set no limit on what he could spend. With their limited income that was quite a concession. In the end she could only brace herself for the reaction which she knew was to come.

It occurred two weeks later, shortly after the start of term. The new head teacher had invited all his staff to a welcoming party at his home. Hilary was relieved to see that, on this occasion, partners were not invited: relations with Mark were still frosty. But the head had made it clear that this was not a formal event – guests were encouraged to come dressed for a relaxing evening. Hilary had a short, black cocktail dress which she had waited a long time to wear. It was just a pity, she thought, that Mark would not be the immediate beneficiary.

It was a good party and went on for a long time. Hilary drank more than she had intended and arrived home well after midnight. Mark was already in bed and fast asleep. It was far too late for a shower. Hilary undressed in the dark and slipped quietly into bed.

It was next morning, as she struggled to wake up in time to go and teach, that Hilary discovered the nature of Mark's revenge. For opening the door of her wardrobe, she was horrified to find just an empty space.

'Where . . . where are all my clothes?' she howled.

'Try the bathroom,' muttered her partner, pretending to be half asleep.

With a sinking feeling she opened the bathroom door and looked into the shower and then the bath. There was plenty of water in the latter. It was also completely full of the contents of her wardrobe. Her three demure dresses, calf-length skirts, modest tops and business suit – in fact, all the clothes she kept for teaching - were sunk beneath the surface.

How much worse could it get? Hilary knelt down and immersed her arm. Yep. It was as she feared. Down below the clothes were the entire contents of her underwear drawer. Angrily she returned to the bedroom and pulled off the duvet from her partner. He blinked at her sleepily but she suspected that he was finding it hard not to guffaw.

'OK, you've had your revenge,' she muttered. 'But I'd say you've overdone it. I've got to go into school today. What the hell am I supposed to wear?'

'I thought teachers could wear whatever they liked.'

'Within reason. I'm not going to teach in my swimming costume.'

'Mm. What about the clothes you were wearing last night?'

'Mark, that was a short, low-cut, slinky black cocktail dress. I teach thirteen-year-old boys and we've just got a new head. Wearing that is not the way to make a good impression.'

But when push came to shove there was little choice. Hilary did her best to make the outfit respectable with a lightweight neck scarf that she found in the hall (which Mark had overlooked) then set out to face the music.

It was clear, though, that the situation at home needed a fuller resolution.

It was after seven before Hilary got home. A chastened Mark had been there since half past six and was cooking chilli con carne – the pick of his limited repertoire. In the cold light of day he'd realised that, in last night's revenge, he'd gone well over the top.

'How was it?' he asked warily, as his partner came into the kitchen.

'Not too bad. The boys were so shocked to see their humdrum teacher dressed like a film star that they actually behaved.'

'Great.' Her partner looked puzzled. 'So did anything go wrong?'

'In a word, Ofsted. You know we've got a new head? He's been here exactly one week. Well, the educational experts decided to settle him in with a surprise inspection. Mine was one of the classes they chose to show him up with.'

'Just as well your kids were under control.'

'I guess. I was the only teacher they saw this morning who got a decent report. I mean, everyone else was hung over from last night's party. So, at lunch time, the head asked me to come with him to entertain the inspectors at the local restaurant. He said I was the only one dressed for the occasion. I think what he meant was that I could seduce them into submission.'

'Yes. I noticed you no longer had the neck scarf.'

'I'm lucky I've still got the dress.'

Hilary reflected for a moment. 'The head must have a special deal with that place: they pulled out all the stops. I reckon the four of us got through six bottles of champagne. By the time we'd finished they were incapable of inspecting anything.'

She smiled. 'I'm in with the new head, anyway. He's asked me to be one of his new assistant heads. But I'm not having any more alcohol for a long time.'

Mark mused for a moment. Was this a chance for reconciliation? 'So all the horrible things I did to you last night . . . they worked out all right in the end?'

Hilary smiled; she was after reconciliation as well. 'Sometimes accidents are bad for us and sometimes they're good. But I think over-reacting to them is never very helpful.'

'You know, I completely agree,' her partner replied.

5.   ASHANTI GOLD

Captain Barton stared out of the cabin of the SS Great Britain across Christiansburg Bay, wishing his bosses in London were less demanding.

'Bring back as much gold as you can,' the signal had ordered. 'With this unrest in the Balkans we must stock up our National Reserves.'

So he'd arrived at the Gold Coast a month before, May 1914, ready to remind the natives of their colonial obligations.

His First Mate, Harry Scrace, had been despatched to Kumasi to negotiate with the Ashantis and bring back the spoil. They had plenty of gold there, it was said; been mining it for centuries. They could easily part with a few crate loads of ingots to satisfy their colonial masters.

Scrace had taken most of the crew with him. Every man had been keen to volunteer: they'd been afloat far too long on the journey back from Australia. Most had never set foot in West Africa. Barton hadn't heard from Scrace since; but that wasn't what was bothering him now.

What disturbed him was the German gunboat he could see across the bay.

He could guess where it had come from: Lomé, the "prettiest town in West Africa" and the capital of Togoland, sixty miles along the coast. Togoland had been annexed by the Germans in 1884, part of the rush for Africa which had seized Europe in the preceding century.

There was a knock at his door; an African entered, wearing

28

hardly a stitch of clothing. It was Kofi, his newly hired servant.

He didn't need to be naked, Barton thought; he'd been offered a Merchant Navy uniform as part of the deal. But there hadn't been much choice, once he'd cut out the candidates that spoke no English. Goodness only knew where Kofi had picked up his variant but it was better than nothing.

'Massa, I have de message from de Commissioner; from de boat over dere.'

The African gestured vaguely out of the cabin porthole. Barton assumed he was pointing at the gunboat.

'Yes, Kofi?'

'De Commissioner, he invite you to dinner on his boat – dis evening.'

This was a surprise. 'Do you know if he speaks English?'

'I tink not a word. But if you take me too, I will interpret for you.'

It wasn't going to be the easiest event of his social calendar but Barton didn't think he could refuse. 'Tell the messenger I am happy to accept the invitation. And that I will bring my African Chief of Staff with me. But I insist, Kofi, that you find some clothes for the occasion.'

The rowing boat set off across the bay at seven; it being the Tropics it was already dark. Kofi, looking incongruous in a Merchant Uniform several sizes too big, took the oars and Barton controlled the rudder. The Captain wondered for a minute whether Kofi was sending him up by his choice of clothing then dismissed the idea: he knew Africans couldn't appreciate European humour.

Twenty minutes later they had reached the gunboat and been welcomed aboard.

The dialogue between the Englishman and the Germans was halting – but could have been worse. Barton was pleased to discover that Kofi spoke passable German as well as English - presumably also a local variant.

The meal was African – yams rather than potatoes, and a groundnut stew. Barton did not dare question what variety of meat had been added. But the Germans, somehow or other, had acquired a crate of French wine which more than compensated - and even seemed to enhance the stilted dialogue.

The conversation, translated back and forth by Kofi, started as follows:

'Herr Barton, your boat is old.'

'Yes, Consul Schmidt. The SS Great Britain was the first iron passenger vessel in the world. Built in 1843 by our great engineer, Isombard Kingdom Brunel. It has sailed to and from Australia many times.'

'Tell me, Captain, what are you carrying on this voyage?'

'As well as a few passengers, we are bringing race horses from South Africa. They breed well there.'

'So why are you berthing on the Gold Coast?'

Barton needed to be careful here. 'My crew have never stayed in this part of Africa. The Ashanti are famous – it took our army several wars to defeat them. They wanted to meet the Ashanti chief. Do not worry, Consul, we will be leaving for England next week.'

The journey back to the SS Great Britain later that evening was not one Barton would wish to repeat. It was a good job the wine fogged his memory. Exhausted and drunk, he could not steer straight; the all-purpose Kofi had had to navigate as well as row.

But once back on board the Captain was delighted to find that the First Mate had returned. Not all the crew, though: several had died of malaria on the journey back from Kumasi. His passengers had seen the signs and were agitating for a swift departure.

Early next morning he met with Scrace in his cabin.

'We have to be careful,' he warned. 'The German gunboat is

watching. I had dinner with their Captain yesterday evening. I did not tell them about the gold but this is Africa; most laws are made up as we go along. They may stop and search us on our way home. How can we hide the gold?'

Kofi was present, once more tidying the cabin; somehow he added himself to the discussion. 'Massa, we Africans have had many years of hiding de gold. De best way is to disguise dem as bricks.'

'And how can we do that?' asked the First Mate dismissively. He didn't like being told what to do by an African.

'De silt here in de harbour is a sort of clay. We coat it round de ingots. Den leave them to dry in de sun for two days. Dey will look and feel like bricks. We load dem back onto de crates, make a tight web of rope around dem and stick dem in de hold.'

'Hm. I suppose, sir, we could give the crates special labels, say they were destined for Freetown?' The First Mate added his contribution.

It was better than just sticking the crates straight in the hold, anyway. Neither Officer had any better ideas.

'Right,' said Barton. 'Let's do that. We'll sail in three days time. But make sure the crew don't pass that on. We'll not leave until it's dark.'

Three days of intense activity later they were ready. Five well-labelled crates of "bricks" had been added to the SS Great Britain's forward hold. Fresh food had been loaded for the crew and more unsullied hay for the horses. Once darkness fell, all lights extinguished, the old iron vessel hauled anchor with the least possible rattling of chains and started, slowly, to chug across the bay.

But despite all their precautions, they were not careful enough. They had not gone far when the lookout, high on the mast above, spied a dark grey shape heading towards them. Then a light, flashing, ordered them to stop.

31

Captain Barton wondered whether to try and outrun the gunboat – for he was sure this was who their challenger was. But his ship was seventy years old; he would never outrun the Germans. Outwardly calm, though inwardly fuming, he ordered his helmsman to stop. A few moments later three small rowing boats traversed the water between the large vessels and then their crew clambered on board.

Although the German Captain spoke no English, he had found two of his crew that could. One of these accosted Barton on the bridge. 'Ze bricks - vere are zey being stored?'

Barton eyed the man's rifle. Should he tell? Then he remembered that his crew knew the location as well. It was likely someone would speak. And even if they all kept silent it wouldn't take their boarders long to search the boat. Bricks were not easy objects to hide.

He decided to pin his hope on the false labelling. But that was a feeble defence.

It took the Germans only a few minutes to clamber into the hold and identify the cargo. The crates were too heavy to take back fully loaded. But the intruders arranged their men in a human chain, back to the rope ladder above their rowing boats. Slowly, one by one, the bricks were passed along the line.

At the ladder a hefty German put the bricks into a large rucksack and then climbed repeatedly up and down, transferring them to the boats.

Meanwhile a second German, armed with a rifle, kept guard.

The whole process took only half an hour. Once the crates' contents had been transferred, the line of Germans broke up; then they re-assembled at the ladder, climbed down and divided themselves between the boats. Slowly – for the bricks were heavy and the boats now low in the water – the three rowing boats and their new cargo started back towards the enemy gunboat.

The SS Great Britain was in the Merchant Navy; it had no cause to carry heavy weapons. But it did carry flares. Captain Barton took his boat to many out-of-the-way parts of the world; he insisted on good safety equipment. Edward Very had invented the flare gun twenty years earlier; now it was a standard piece of equipment.

'If we've not got the gold let's make sure the Germans haven't either,' Barton observed to Scrace. He gave an order.

The First Mate was a practised user of the flare gun. Swiftly he loaded it, dropped to his knees, and took aim. The Germans had not yet gone twenty yards: they were a sitting target.

Bang! There was a flash in the bottom of the first boat then a glugging sound. One or two Germans gave a shout of panic. The boat started to take on board more water and then, slowly, to sink.

The First Mate took aim again. Two more shots and two more successes.

Captain Barton turned to his helmsman. 'Full steam ahead.'

Slowly the Great Britain started to move away. The Captain had no intention of providing the Germans, all now thrashing about in the sea, with life belts. He certainly wouldn't want any of them back on board. And he needed the gunboat to take as long as possible on their rescue.

The Great Britain was not the fastest ship in the world but once out of sight he knew she would be hard to find. And there was no reason, anyway, for the Germans to chase them. All the gold was now at the bottom of the ocean.

'It's such a pity we lost all that gold,' Barton said to Kofi, as the African served dinner in his cabin that evening.

The African smiled. 'Massa, why you tink de gold is all in de bricks?'

'That's what you suggested, Kofi. That's what you did, isn't it?'

'But Massa, dat is a well-known African trick. Many others knew it besides me. So I knew it was not safe. No, de gold is hidden under de straw, next to de horses.'

He continued, 'But dere may yet be more trouble on de way.

33

You tink, maybe, we shouldn't tell de crew until we reach South-ampton?'

The SS Great Britain still has a life today as a floating museum in Bristol.

6.   FRENCH CONNECTION

The smart, portly man, with a sheet of paper in his hand, strutted to the front of the stage. 'As Returning Officer for the seat of Thanet South, I hereby declare the votes counted are as follows.'

Back in the television studio, the equally smartly-dressed Huw Edwards turned once more to his guests. It was eight thirty in the morning, the end of a long night. 'Here we go, Nick: boom or bust?'

'It's another tight one,' Nick Robinson replied hoarsely. He prayed his doctor wasn't watching: the medic had told him he needed another month off to recover from the operation - but who wanted to watch politics at home when you could be commentating on it live? 'UKIP have got four million votes overall,' he whispered, 'but will their elected leader become an Member of Parliament?'

Before he could develop the point the Returning Officer started his announcement.

'Jennings Armstrong, Conservative: 11,629.' A scattering of applause echoed around the assembly hall: it was a lot, but would it be enough?

'Pinky Braithwaite, Labour: 8,417.' Less applause this time. No-one had expected a Labour win.

'Nigel Farage, UK Independence Party: 12,643.' There was cheering from a raucous section of the Hall, matched by boos from elsewhere. Farage, it seemed, had beaten his main opponent, though he'd made as many enemies as friends. Oddly, he did not look too happy.

The Returning Officer continued. The Liberal Democrats and the Greens had, in Thanet as elsewhere, lost their deposits. The Monster Raving Loony Party had created even less work for the vote counters. Finally he reached the last name on the list.

'Nigelle Fromage, Big Cheese Activist: 14,206.' A huge grin spread across the face of the attractive, thirty five year old candidate as she gave a twirl and punched the air in delight. There was a stunned silence around the hall and in the studio.

'So I hereby declare Nigelle Fromage to be the duly elected Member for this constituency.'

As the candidates on stage started the ritual of shaking hands, offered with a mixture of emotions, Huw Edwards turned to his expert.

'My hearing aid's on the wobble, Nick. I don't think I heard that right?'

Nick Robinson was paid to have instant wisdom on the latest electoral whims, expected or not. 'Even on this night of massive shocks, Huw, from the north of Scotland to the southwest of England, this is perhaps the biggest shock of all. I confess I'd never heard of the Big Cheese Activists – perhaps they emerged last month, while I was ill. But they're a force to be reckoned with here. They – or to be more precise, she - could be just what the Conservatives need to drag themselves over the line.'

'If her views are in line with theirs, of course, Nick. That's not guaranteed – she looks quite sane. But if she's beaten Farage that should do her some good with Cameron's minders.'

Robinson had been keeping his eye on the television pictures. 'Hold that thought for a minute, Huw, she's moved forward to give her "thank you" speech. Maybe that'll give us a clue.'

It might have done had she chosen to speak in English. But her French was too rapid for the rusty linguistic skills of Nick or Huw. Fortunately Emily Maitlis, managing the latest jazzed-up results screen behind them, had finished her education in this century and was able to translate.

'Madame Fromage says she thanks the Returning Officer for the efforts of the counting staff and the proletariat of South Thanet for their support. She promises to represent all Thanetians in Parliament . . . and to lobby hard for a "yes" to Europe in the forthcoming referendum. She says it's only thanks to the European Union that she's been able to settle in the UK, so a vote for her has to be a vote for Europe.'

There was a pause while the newly elected MP flicked her chic scarf and completed her address; then Maitlis again translated: 'She says it's been a particular joy to fight and win this campaign against Monsieur Farage. She advises him to take a break from politics.'

As Maitlis was translating, Edwards had been watching events on the stage. 'I'm not sure if he picked that up. He heard the word "Farage" and then started smiling inanely.'

'He's only been a European MP for twenty years,' said fount-of-all-knowledge Robinson. 'With their short parliamentary sessions and all his time spent in the UK as leader of UKIP you can't expect him to be there long enough to learn French. That's probably one reason why he wants to get us out of Europe.'

Edwards had been wrestling with his earpiece. 'Nick, I've just been reminded that we have a reporter down in Thanet. Let's go over to her.'

Jo Coburn's cheerful face appeared. 'Well, that's certainly a turn up for the book, Huw. Locals tell me that in their experience Farage is one of those characters for whom a small amount goes a long way. So the longer he spent here, the more the enthusiasm for him dropped: his popularity wasn't as high as you might expect. He had one or two struggles in this campaign – there was an ugly scene the other night outside the Red Lion when an angry crowd assembled and Farage was stuck inside.'

'Hardly a problem for him, surely?' asked Nick.

'Even so, that's one story the television cameras missed,' added Huw. 'How come pictures of that didn't make the national press, Jo?'

'I'm told he was smuggled away from the pub next morning in a large rubbish bag. That certainly avoided the press photos. The trouble was, it's alleged, the bag was then picked up by the dustbin men: he only just managed to avoid being dumped in the local refuse tip. That put him off drinking in the town.'

'Hm. All that might explain why he didn't do better. But how did Madame Fromage do so well?'

'It's no coincidence that she came to Thanet with a similar name. Changed for the purpose, no doubt. Literacy is low in this part of the world and to the casual voter Nigelle sounds more fashionable than Nigel. You may have noticed she was the only female candidate. I'm sure that swayed plenty of men who might otherwise have voted Farage.'

'That's not the only thing, surely?'

'Well, no. But she is also a jazz singer. She's been performing in one or other local pub with her ensemble every night from well before the campaign started - while giving out handouts to each member of each appreciative audience. I caught up with her two nights ago; she's got a deep, husky voice. Someone told me she was also subsidising the price of beer on the nights when she performed.'

'That must have cost someone a fair bit. Where's she been staying?'

'I don't know all the details, Huw, but I'm told she's lodged with the editor of the local paper. So he's given her strong support. And I reckon the French government have got some sort of slush fund to help her campaign. I mean, the French have no reason to want a successful Nigel Farage inside our Parliament, have they?'

A month later the same team were back to cover the State Opening of Parliament. 'And what a month it's been, Huw,' wheezed Nick Robinson, wishing he too had managed a month off in Ibiza.

'Some of our viewers may have switched off after the election, Nick. Bring 'em up to date.'

'Well, Huw, you may remember there was one moment, just after the election, when the result looked clear: Conservatives back in power with a small majority. Duncan Smith rolling up his sleeves to battle on with universal credit, George Osborne aiming to vacuum-pack the state. But you know these pollsters: they'd predicted minority government and that was what most people wanted – the right wing of the Tory party, anyway.'

'So what happened?'

'My sources tell me that David Cameron took a bit of a shine to Nigelle. He could speak French, of course, which put him at an advantage over most of his cabinet colleagues now that Hague had gone. A morning of private talks, a stroll in the spring sunshine down to a Whitehall bistro, and Nigelle Fromage found herself appointed Foreign Secretary in the new administration.

'"This'll show Europe we mean business about renegotiation," the Prime Minister declared, as the two stood on the steps of Downing Street, beaming at the cameras. Nigelle certainly added some much-needed glamour to his government. "It's ten steps up on Eric Pickles," one reporter was heard to remark. "And ten stone down on the weight count," his colleague replied.

'Unfortunately,' Robinson went on, 'the appointment did not meet with universal acclaim. The Tory Right weren't that stupid. They could see this was a backdoor way of making sure the Europe Referendum, when it came, would result in a massive "yes". So a dozen Tories declined the whip and declared themselves "independents".

'With the result that Cameron's majority lasted for all of forty eight hours and since then, as our exit poll predicted, he's back to being a minority government.' Robinson grinned. 'These polls are smart – you have to admit.'

'It's not all bad news, then.'

'There are certainly compensations, Huw. For example, in terms of style, Ms Fromage is at least a match for Ms Sturgeon when it comes to dealing with Scotland – big cheese stands up to small fish. But Ms Fromage has the further advantage that she can sing like an angel.'

Edwards was eyeing his television monitor. 'The Queen leaves the Palace and her procession is setting off down the Mall. Unless a wheel comes off nothing will happen for some time. Nick, remind us how her singing came to light.'

'In a word, Huw, Andrew Marr.'

'That's two words.' Edwards was not as clever as his expert but he could count.

'Because of the rumpus in the Conservatives, and Miliband trying to reappoint himself as shadow Foreign Secretary so he could have personal briefings with Ms Fromage, there was a gap on Marr's show. So at short notice Nigelle filled in the final section with her jazz band. No-one remembered the show but everyone remembered the singer. Ms Fromage was signed up on her way out of the BBC as an instant replacement for Jools Holland. She's been performing every Friday night since.'

'Gives party politicals a bit of a boost then.'

Edwards was keeping up with his monitor and could report some action. 'The Queen is just entering Parliament. And there are the MP's, jostling to squash into the Lords, with Nigelle Fromage just behind David Cameron. The start of the next chequered chapter of British politics, Nick?'

'That's right, Huw. I'd say it's a step on from democracy to benign dictatorship. A triumph, perhaps, for the British gift of compromise?'

7.   DONE IT YESTERDAY

Recently-retired Henry Grimthorpe didn't just dislike DIY, he hated it with a vengeance. His passion, though not yet a cause for celebration, was for his writing. He lived for his Writers' Circle, which met every Thursday evening in the town-centre library.

In contrast his wife, Maria, ten years younger, despised poetry but loved pattern. She delighted in mixing the most outlandish colours, whether on fresh, vibrant curtain fabric or in contrasting wallpaper, in every room and on every wall of their modest terraced home. She chose all the colours herself. It was just a pity that she was colour-blind.

Maria was not personally a Damage-it-Yourself activist. Her skills lay in managing her husband as she directed him from room to room - then in calling in a relevant expert to redress the damage as each new problem emerged. It was a costly business — not just funding the workmen's time but also the hush money she paid, to make sure word of the remedial effort never got out. For Maria was a proud woman: she liked to boast ad nauseam to her friends about her husband's decorating endeavours. To the outside world they seemed like a dream couple.

It had taken years for Henry to persuade his wife to limit the DIY to one room at a time. 'You women have the hormones for multitasking,' he had observed, 'we men can only do one thing at once.'

'If that,' she was tempted to retort. But not out loud. She had long ago realised that it had been a mistake to take on Henry at all. She'd later warned the vicar that marriage preparation classes ought to include a trial on home decoration, so you could spot the dud before it was too late.

The current focus of DIY was the kitchen. Maria had spotted slate tiles on special offer in Wickes and now wanted to cook in a pseudo-Cornish kitchen. By now Henry had given up arguing. It took all his energies to make the changes she wanted, without a row about whether they were needed.

Though they'd lived in the house for many years, this was the first time the pair had lifted the kitchen lino. It was a shock to discover that much of the wood underneath had been providing a very long lunch to a colony of woodworm.

'That's all right, we'll eat out until you've done,' she counselled, a pleasant idea but one that put extra time pressure on his efforts. The Harlequin, just along the road, was not a cheap place to eat.

So Henry set to work. Out came a layer of plywood and then plank after plank of rotten wood; the hole beneath the kitchen grew deeper and deeper. Eventually he reached a layer of mouldy leaves but it was clear this was not strong enough to take the weight of a slate floor. A concrete foundation would be needed and a delivery of ready-mix was ordered. 'It'll arrive next week.'

It was about this time that Henry, returning early from his Writers' Circle after overlooking the Christmas break, realised that Maria was having an affair. The first clue was the white tradesman's van parked outside, owned by W J Higgins. Henry thought nothing of it at the time, but decided he would inject some surprise into his wife's life by coming home quietly and early.

It was as he stepped into the hall that he heard the noise of conversation from the bedroom upstairs. He hadn't heard Maria giggle like that for many years; the lower voice she was responding to sounded like its owner was having a good time as well. Henry paused to listen, wondered for a moment about barging in and then discretion prevailed. Silently he slipped out from the home that had taken so much of his energies and down to the Harlequin.

As he nursed his drink, Henry felt first shock and then betrayal.

42

For a long time he had felt exploited; slowly the feelings turned from jealousy to rage. What should he do?

One option would be to pretend he'd heard nothing, wait an hour and then go home. But how would he contain his feelings – either when he first saw his wife or in the days that followed?

No, he had to do something. So suppose he confronted Maria; and she confessed and sought his forgiveness? Even if he could accept that, how would he be sure that the affair was over and wouldn't start all over again?

How many more remedial workmen did she know?

He could just walk out for good; but where would he go? The trouble was that his wife, with her skills in health care, was their main source of income. Their home was jointly owned but his retirement income was meagre. He'd been unemployed too often to build up much of a pension.

Henry brooded for a long time trying to find a solution.

By the time he was home, the white van was no longer outside and his wife was in the bath, no doubt removing traces of an extra presence in the home. Little was said, though a lot on both sides went unspoken.

One week later, the ready-mixed concrete arrived and was dumped at the front door in mid afternoon. Henry had a lot to do before he could head off for his Writers' Circle.

He'd planned to use a wheelbarrow to transfer the soggy concrete into the kitchen, but Maria's veto had been decisive. So it was a long afternoon of trudging through the hall with the material in a bucket. Slowly, bucket by bucket, the space under the kitchen floor was filled.

The firm where he had ordered the concrete had warned him, 'It'll take a long time to set in the cold weather.' The surface was still fluid when he said goodbye to Maria and set out for his Writers' Circle.

Henry had a busy evening ahead. The first step, as he hurried down the street, was to find the alleyway which allowed access to his back garden. He wasn't used to this sort of activity - he wished he'd brought his torch. Eventually he reached his garden, slipped across it and in through the back door. He listened: there was silence from within.

Next he reached down and shifted the plank which he had carefully set above the liquid concrete. After that he shinned up the cupboard and reached for the fuse box above. He'd studied this earlier and had found by trial and error which fuse controlled the downstairs lighting.

Finally he settled himself and pulled out his phone.

'Hello Maria,' he began, speaking softly. 'I'm at the bus stop. I've just remembered something.'

'Henry, let me guess – you've forgotten your poem again.'

'Don't be silly, it's not that serious. I'd come back if it was. The thing is, I realised I never locked the back door after I'd finished putting down the concrete.'

'You're a bumbling idiot. Thanks for telling me, anyway. Don't worry, I'll make sure it's sorted.'

Now was the critical moment. Henry tensed himself: timing was everything. He seized the fuse and prepared to switch off all the downstairs lights, precisely as the kitchen door opened.

There was a muttered curse in the pitch darkness; then the woman stepped forward onto the plank – or rather, where the plank should have been.

There was a thud as she tripped and fell onto the pliable concrete surface. Followed by an angry muffled scream as Henry, sliding off the cupboard, pushed her head deep into the soggy material.

Five minutes later the sounds of protest had ceased. Henry gingerly climbed back onto the work surface and reset the fuse. Then once more he crouched down and smoothed the floor surface, this time pushing down and fully covering the body.

Half an hour later Henry was sitting once more in the Harlequin, nursing his pint and working out his next part in the drama. Maria only worked at the start of the week so it would be several days before she was missed. He needed a plausible story as to where she had gone – distant relatives, maybe? And careful timing on when he alerted the police. Not until the concrete was set, any-way.

It was just after ten when he returned home.

'Hello dear, I'm back,' he called. It was important, he'd decided, to voice all his lines. He had a role to fulfil when the police started their enquiries: rehearsal would help.

So it came as a complete shock, as he stepped into the hall, to hear the familiar voice calling from the bedroom. 'Henry, is that you?'

'Maria?' he stammered. Was it a ghost? His conscience stirred. Would he never be rid of her memory? Would she still force his DIY, even from beyond the grave?

He turned on the hall light. His wife came downstairs in her nightdress, looking pale and shaken.

'Maria, whatever's the matter?'

'After you rang I never got as far as the back door. Then I heard something – or someone. I was terrified: I thought, once they've got in, they've a choice: to ravish me or to run off with the house-hold trinkets. So I went back to bed, locked the bedroom door and kept as still as a mouse. I've been there ever since. Thank heavens you're home.'

And stepping forward, she gave him the biggest hug he'd had for years.

That might have sounded convincing, thought Henry, but there had been some woman in the kitchen. If that wasn't Maria, who on earth was it?

In the days that followed a new stage began in their relationship. Maria seemed less demanding and the DIY, apparently, less urgent.

Henry had tensed himself to kill once. That had given him some self confidence and a new willingness to counter his wife's suggestions. But he didn't think he could try it again. He certainly didn't want to dig up and relay the kitchen concrete.

The slate tiles looked remarkably solid. Both parties, in their different ways, had good reason to leave them undisturbed.

Wendy Jane Higgins would rest in peace.

8. EAMONN'S TALE

A hideous whine followed by a massive bang wrenched the evening air.

'What the hell was that?' asked Eamonn Stothard, to no-one in particular, in the ensuing silence.

Swiftly the gangling, bespectacled Irishman followed his land-lady, Mary Buchanan, out of the small house and down the drive. Just this side of the road they could see a young woman, dressed in army uniform, lying trapped, half underneath a motor bike. She was moaning in pain. The engine had stalled but the small head-light was still flickering and gave some limited illumination.

A shocked Mrs Buchanan put her hand to her mouth. 'Eamonn, it's Molly,' she said. 'Can you manage to lift up the bike? I'll try to help the girl.'

It was a struggle but eventually the bike was moved sideways and Molly released. She was not as badly injured as they'd feared, though she had nasty scrapes along her left arm and knee. Her uniform, too, looked in need of urgent repair.

Between them they escorted her into the house, Eamonn taking most of the weight from her left side. 'Sit her down,' ordered the landlady, 'I'll go and make us all a cup of tea.'

Eamonn was left with the congenial task of comforting the vic-tim. She was a pretty girl beneath the pain, he guessed in her early twenties. 'What happened there, Molly? Can you remember?'

'I was going too fast round that final corner. I was tired - I've had a bloody long drive. The bike just seemed to skid from under me.' Suddenly her face contorted in alarm. 'Hell, I hope the ma-chine's alright. It's military issue.' She started to struggle out of the

47

chair.

'Stay still, I'll go and look in a minute,' said Eamonn, in his reassuring brogue. 'They build 'em pretty strong these days, it should be OK. You don't have any panniers or anything you need fetching?'

'No, I'd already been to the Park, thank you. Blast, I guess I just lost concentration on that final bend.'

Although the two had been in the same accommodation for over a year they had shared nothing of their wartime lives. "Mum's the word" and "Careless talk costs lives" had been drummed into them. Asking questions was equally frowned on. But for a few minutes Molly's accident and Eamonn's part in her subsequent rescue seemed to lift the security blanket.

'How far'd you been?' he asked.

'Thurso. It's the far north of Scotland,' replied Molly. 'Seven hundred miles.' Eamonn was Irish; she mustn't take his geography for granted. She remembered she'd had no idea where Thurso was when she was first sent there.

'Yes,' she went on, 'I started back last night; soon after midnight. Drove through the night to an army camp on the Scottish border. Slept for an hour then came on back here. Travelling at night was safer, they said.' She sniffed to show her contempt for the advice. The person who'd offered it had not had to cope with the cold or the isolation.

'With not a single streetlight to help? And no extra protection from the cold? You poor kid; no wonder you're shattered.' He mused. 'What on earth needs bringing that far – and that quickly?'

'I've no idea. I guess it must be important to someone. We're not playing a game, you know. With all the rationing, petrol's in very short supply.'

Mrs Buchanan returned at that point and their newly-discovered closeness was put on hold. 'Here's some tea, my luvs. And as it's an emergency I've broken into next week's biscuits.

Help yourself, Molly, then Eamonn and I will start on the First Aid.'

Over the next few weeks Eamonn's friendship with Molly started to grow. Mrs Buchanan insisted that the girl was not fit to go to work next morning; Eamonn was tasked with reporting her absence to the Park authorities. It was not out of his way; he'd been a maintenance man on the site before the war had even started. But he'd never been inside the administration block.

The Irishman was amazed by the complexity of the operation. Women seemed to be largely in control. He'd had to queue to be allowed in, then interviewed to explain himself and finally forced to queue again to leave his message. His own pass showed Mrs Buchanan's address as his place of lodging. Eventually someone recognised that Molly Filbert was living at the same address as he was, so his knowledge of her accident made sense.

It made a good tale to tell the girl when he returned home that evening.

Molly had been dosed with aspirins, slept most of the day and was looking a lot better. Mrs Buchanan had been a nurse before the war and had the girl's various scrapes all neatly bandaged.

'I'll be ready to go back to the Park tomorrow,' Molly told him. Eamonn wondered whether to dissuade her then decided it would do no good. War-time imperative ruled all of their lives.

The wall of separation between them, though, had been breached. Eamonn now found himself regularly in Molly's room – initially to check she was recovering from her injuries, then to swap asides on their often-mundane days in the Park, finally to share more personal details. Mrs Buchanan, while not overjoyed by the burgeoning friendship, took no active steps to prevent it.

Eamonn gathered that there was a rota governing trips to Thurso, with Molly on once a week; other girls covered the other days. Whatever came from Thurso needed to be brought every day. Molly clearly did not know – did not ask – what it was that needed moving with so much effort. And he was careful not to ask her questions which she was unable to answer.

But for anyone – most of all a spirited young woman like Molly – keeping quiet about everyday happenings in their lives, for week after week, is practically impossible. Life has to be shared with someone.

On the Park there were security personnel to enforce a discipline of silence but this did not apply in their lodgings. Mary Buchanan was fierce enough in her way but she was not security. Without much prompting, Molly found herself sharing observations and misgivings, joys and complaints, with her fellow-lodger. Eamonn proved himself a good listener.

Eamonn's ground pass did not allow him access to any of the huts. It had been made clear at the start of the war that he was there for maintenance and to help build the new huts as they were required. That kept him very busy; it was amazing how new huts kept being needed.

But Molly's work, when she wasn't motoring to and from Scotland, required her to move packets from hut to hut. She didn't know what the packets contained but she started to wonder what was going on inside the different huts. Eamonn never asked her questions but he was willing to comment on whatever she told him. Exchanging hard information was strictly forbidden; but swapping speculation, between two people who knew almost nothing, could scarcely be suppressed in the same way.

The official story was that the Park was one of many administration centres scattered across the country; the vast majority of personnel were women, mostly young and nearly all in uniform.

Eamonn found it hard to accept this. If it was administration it was being done with extreme intensity. Molly had just one day off per week and worked ten hours a day on the rest (more on her trips to the far north). He'd observed that she had had just one weekend's leave in the past six months; and he gathered this was the usual ration for all her colleagues.

For an administrative centre the workforce seemed to be remarkably well cared for. There was a canteen and a theatre; a small lake filled the centre and the main building was a Victorian mansion. Not all British administrative centres could be pampered like this, surely?

Then came the rumour that within the next few weeks the Park would have an important visitor. Eamonn could have remained to see who it was; but he decided that further delay was unnecessary.

Instead of attending the Park he set out for the main railway station in the town. His doctored pass was accepted and he bought a ticket to Liverpool. Two days later, aided by a sad story of an ill uncle in Wicklow and a supporting letter giving the melancholy details, he was on the weekly ferry to Dublin.

A day later Eamonn Stothard was in a safe house, telling his minder all he knew about the Park, where he had worked for four years. It sounded like this might be very important. Two weeks later he was in a U-boat, being transferred back to Keil on the way to seeing his honorary uncle, Admiral Karl Donitz, in Berlin.

'Good to see you, my boy,' said the soon-to-be appointed Commander of the German Navy. 'Tell me, what have you learned on the matter we discussed all those years ago?'

'I began with a calculated guess, uncle. If there was a place being set up for decryption, the people to run it – the UK's best mathematicians - would come from Cambridge or Oxford. There is just one branch line joining the two; I considered the towns along it. There was one town where this line intersected the main railway line from London to the Northwest – at a place called Bletchley. And Bletchley is almost exactly midway between the two University towns.'

'Never heard of it,' said the Admiral dismissively.

'Precisely, uncle. A small, obscure town would be ideal for the purpose.'

'So you went to have a look?'

'I arrived there from Southern Ireland in 1938. There was an estate – with a park and a lake - not three hundred metres from the station. I got a job as gardener. Then the place was taken over by government and a big fence erected round it. They said it was a new administration centre.'

'It could have been,' grunted the Admiral. 'In the run-up to war they'd want to move as much as they could out of London.'

'I had lodgings three kilometres away with an old lady. A year later, with the outset of the war, new people started to arrive. I had a fellow lodger called Molly, also based at Bletchley Park.'

'If it was anything to do with decryption, security would be very tight?'

'It was. For the first year she never said anything. But every Thursday Molly came back very late, on a motor bike. So I decided to shake things up. One Thursday evening, after it was dark, I soaked the drive with oil.'

The Admiral mused for a moment, then it made sense. He grinned. 'To cause her to skid?'

'Exactly. It worked beautifully – brought us much closer together. Her weekly trip, I discovered, was bringing a parcel from the north of Scotland. Slowly I started to learn about the Park and what might be going on. '

'How big is this Park? What are the staff numbers?'

'There must be several thousand. Nearly all of them women.'

The admiral's interest dropped imperceptibly away. He sighed.

'Women, eh. It can't be the decoding centre then. Sounds like an administration block after all. Well tried, lad. But for the future we'd better find a smarter way.'

9. LOOE'S CHANGE

Toby Hammond, journalist on probation for a major National broadsheet, sniffed and sighed. There was no significant smell, anyway. He couldn't see much water on the main street – the pavements were clear - but maybe that meant only the side streets had suffered damage?

This was his first solo outing; he was desperate to make an impact. His colleagues in Bristol had warned him that Looe was the "flood capital of Cornwall" and the young journalist had been sent down to tell the latest tale. All he needed was some hard evidence that he could report on.

It was past midnight, a dark night, but even so his camera was poised to depict the drama. If it ever happened, he thought – this felt more like "Waiting for Godot".

Suddenly he noticed the lights were still on in the Co-op. The shop was open: they certainly hung on to catch their customers here. The clock on the tower opposite showed half past twelve. Given that it was early February, the tourist season didn't begin until April and the town had just suffered the worst storm of the winter, this seemed like optimism on stilts.

But could this be his story? Toby sidled up to the shop's doorway and looked in.

Inside a short, middle-aged Asian woman with a yellow headscarf (he couldn't tell her background more precisely) seemed to be sweeping – no, it was mopping - the floor. Perhaps he'd discovered that the Co-op, too, exploited immigrant labour? Maybe they were no more ethical than anybody else? Probably her minder was somewhere close by: he'd better be careful.

Idiot! This was England, he reminded himself. It might be late but there was no need to be afraid. Toby gave the glass door a gentle push and was slightly surprised when he found it unlocked. He'd been taught by his newspaper to identify and interview as many disaster witnesses as he could. 'That was the only way,' they'd said, 'to get the whole picture.'

Toby knew he'd arrived in Looe very late. This was the only person he'd found; so must be the place to start.

'Good evening, sir. And how are you?' The woman had looked up as he stepped inside and stopped her mop work for a moment. Her accent sounded an odd mixture of Asian and Cornish. Toby deduced that she must have been living here for some time.

'Good evening,' he replied, 'you're working very late tonight.'

'It's the floods, sir. We have to clean everything up, ready to open again tomorrow morning.'

'I'm a journalist – my name is Toby, Toby Hammond. I've been sent down to cover the floods. They're supposed to be bad at the moment.'

'Very bad, sir. That's what they tell us, anyway. Looe was on the top item on the BBC news this evening. They made the place look dreadful.'

'Yes. I saw the news before I set off. That's why I drove down this evening. I'm here to catch the event for my newspaper.'

'Very good, sir, very good. I wish you luck.'

Toby wasn't quite sure why he needed luck. It was just journalistic competence, surely? Find the flood, film the damage, file the report; then forget and move on.

The English public had been told by the BBC that there were floods in Cornwall. They already knew that the county had been "completely shut off from the rest of the country" when the railway line had been washed away round Dawlish. Toby had been slightly surprised to find he could still drive down here.

He knew the more literate members of the public would expect to read all about the floods in next morning's newspaper. Tabloid readers would be content to see a few pictures before turning to ogle at an inside page.

'You've lived in Looe for a while?' he asked.

'Twenty six years, sir. It's a very nice place. Not too wet, anyhow.'

Toby fiddled with his camera. He was conscious that he needed to get on. 'So where should I go, would you say, to find the worst of the floods?'

'Bangladesh, sir. They have good floods there – almost every year. The media do a terrific job covering those.'

'I'm sorry,' said Toby. He'd got crossed wires, somehow. 'What's your name, please? And are you from Bangladesh?'

'I'm Samira, sir, Samira Choudhuri. And yes, I'm from Dhaka.' The woman gave a ghost of a smile. 'We always say that's the Bangladeshi sister town to Looe.'

Was that a joke? He couldn't be sure. Toby Hammond had never taken much interest in disasters abroad: they seemed a long way away. He'd never taken geography that seriously in his school days. Dimly he remembered something about the place, at the end of the news, a few months back.

'Oh. Am I right, our news carried pictures of a helicopter, rescuing people from the roofs of their houses? Amidst miles and miles of water, stretching as far as the eye could see.'

'I think, sir, that you saw a staged event. We only have two working helicopters, you see, in the Ganges Delta. The rest are broken. We can't afford the spare parts – not at the prices the West want to charge. So the camera was being flown in one of them, filming the other one as it did a token rescue. There are always plenty of submerged huts to choose from. Whole villages, towns even. Most of the people sitting on roofs just have to stay there until they run out of drinkable water. Then they collapse, slide off the roof and drown.'

Samira laughed, bitterly. 'Your media aren't so keen to show that bit, of course.'

Toby wasn't sure where this encounter was going or whether he wanted to go on with it. He could see that, for some reason, the woman looked upset. He couldn't just walk out.

'You sound like you've seen the reality first hand?'

'My family lived in the wettest part of the country. Every year, though, we managed to survive – we had a small boat we could take shelter in until the waters went down. Then, one year, I wasn't at home, I was staying with my aunt in Dhaka. I was a teenager, you see, completing my education. I would talk to my family every week on the telephone. One day they told me, in a panic, that the family boat had sprung a leak. It was soon afterwards that the monsoon began. And next week . . . no-one was there to answer my call.'

Samira was almost in tears now. She gave a snuffle then continued. 'Eventually I heard that all my family had been drowned. That's when my aunt pulled all the strings she could to send me to the UK. I've been here ever since.'

Toby Hammond did not know what to say. He was a young man from a comfortable, middle-class background and well out of his depth. Samira had come to the end of her tale and was watching him carefully. Was she after some charity or something? How much should he give? What was the going rate, he wondered, to someone who's lost their whole family?

Or was she just hoping to see a small sign of compassion?

'Can you advise me, please, Samira, where's the best place to go to see some evidence of flooding? Here, tonight, in Looe? I need some pictures, you see, for my newspaper. That's my job.' He was conscious, as he spoke, that these floods here could not possibly compare with those in Bangladesh. But this was what he'd come for tonight, the project he'd been assigned.

'If you'd been here at ten o'clock you might have seen some-

56

thing,' she replied. 'There's just one street in Looe where it looks dramatic, next to the quay. The BBC knows where to put its cameras to best effect and what parts to hide. They get the same flood warning we do. That's why they come back here every year – it's nice and close, you see, to BBC Plymouth. But I'm afraid, now, tonight, you're too late. The water in the streets here only lasts a couple of hours.'

Toby looked at her, shocked. Two hours? For the flood capital of Cornwall? The woman must be joking. But looking at her carefully, he could see that she was serious.

'So what about the water that's got inside the shops?'

'We're used to it. All the shops and cafés in Looe have tiled floors. No carpets here, thank you. And we make sure, when we hear a flood warning, that none of our stock is piled on the floor. It's just seawater, you see, not raw sewage or anything. It washes through the place and then it's gone.'

Samira turned back and drained her mop. 'I've nearly finished mopping up here. By tomorrow morning it'll all have dried and we'll be back in business.'

Toby Hammond could see there were more lessons here in Looe about the world of the media than there were about floods. Internationally speaking, Looe was far from being a flood disaster. But could the world cope with the less sensational truth?

'Samira, would you mind if I took a picture of you mopping up?' asked Toby. 'And would you give me permission to retell your story? If people really want to know about floods – serious floods – then you're the one with the story to tell.'

Pebbles on the shore

Looe at high tide in early September. The Cornish Conundrum, **"Looe's Connections"** *tells a longer tale based around the effects of flooding.*

10. ELECTION-NIGHT SPECIAL

Ten pm, May 7th 2015. The exit poll had just appeared on the television on the wall behind the bar, leading to a stunned, unbelieving silence in the crowded Whitehall saloon.

'You couldn't make it up,' observed the London Pride, who'd just made his way to one of the rear alcoves, to the Fosters Lager who was the other occupant of the tiny table.

'Don't you believe it,' replied the Fosters, a brash-suited man with what sounded like a colonial twang. 'Making it up is what all these pollsters do – in fact, given the fickleness of public opinion, it's all they can do. But if newspapers will pay for the results – as is the current fashion - that's all the pollsters need.'

The Pride was far from convinced. 'But all those polls – for weeks and weeks – have predicted a hung Parliament. Now we've got this final one - and it's telling us the Tories are well ahead. It's completely contradictory. What're we supposed to believe?'

'Come on, mate, what d'you want to believe?'

'Well, I'd fallen for the polls,' said the Pride. 'I was expecting weeks of confusion, with no-one in charge. I mean, if the electorate don't back anyone then maybe we should have a couple of years of parliamentary hibernation. Lay off the MPs, close down the Houses of Parliament, put their salaries into restoring the building and re-run the election in, say, 2018. It wouldn't do the MPs any harm to experience unemployment. They're keen enough to inflict it on the rest of us.'

He looked at his new companion. 'Did you know, Belgium recently managed without a government for two whole years? Didn't seem to do them much harm.'

The Foster's pondered for a moment. 'But how could you tell? I mean, the only famous Belgian I know is that detective – Hercule Poirot - and he hasn't solved a case for half a century. At least, not one that's been reported. This "first past the post" scheme you've got here may be archaic and crazy but it generally gets you a result.'

It sounded like the Fosters man had some expertise on this polling business. Apart from Sunderland Central – where, it was said, they weighed the vote rather than counted them – David Dimbleby had just told them there wouldn't be any firm election results until midnight. They were both likely to be here for some time; the Pride decided to learn what he could.

'If it's as random as all that, how come all these newspaper polls have been giving the same result?'

The Fosters took a swig of his lager and then started to explain. 'Well. You do realise that the first set of numbers from a poll – the raw data - is nothing like the published outcome?'

'Huh. You mean they fiddle the figures?'

'In a way, I suppose. Mainly because in any poll – except the exit poll – there are huge numbers of "undecideds" – maybe 30%. So, one way or another, these blank answers have to be removed.'

'You mean, to avoid the "undecideds" leading the polls week after week? That would dent the headlines a bit. "No-one is preferred to Cameron", "Miliband is worse than anyone at all", and so on.'

'Precisely.'

'So how do they do that?'

'Well, in the early days they would just assume that these people wouldn't actually vote. Or else – which comes to the same thing - that they'd eventually come to much the same decisions as those who've been prepared to give you their views already.'

'Trouble is, that's a big assumption,' observed the Pride. He had professional reasons for keeping track of poll findings.

'Quite. So, more recently, academics have come up with re-finements. For example, you can allow for "shy Tories", and as-sume that, say, a quarter of any set of "undecideds" are actually Tories – but ones who like to keep their views to themselves. Or, if you happen to know the ages of your interview panel, you can as-sume that if they're under, say, thirty, they won't vote anyway.'

The Pride wanted to show he could see where his companion was heading. 'Or . . . you could allow for "lazy Labour" and assume that only 80% of their intending voters would actually bother to turn out. The rest would stay with their ferrets in the Dog and Duck. But the key thing, then, is the ratios. How'd you get the fac-tors to apply?'

It turned out that his companion was from Down Under. 'There are studies from Australia that I brought over a couple of years ago. I did my level best to make sure all the pollsters here were aware of them. There are plenty of my fellow-Aussies employed by polling companies and they all like a drink.'

The Fosters raised his glass and gave a laugh. 'That's probably why their results are so similar.'

There was something not quite right here. The Pride decided he had to delve further.

'The polls were not just similar – the two parties neck and neck – but the exit poll we've just seen suggests they were all wrong. So in fact your adjustment factors weren't any good.'

The Pride was taking a sip of his drink when a further thought struck him. 'Hey – you lot are forced to vote, aren't you? It's poll-ing booth or police cell. So how could any of your factors make sense over here?'

'I did realise that,' said the Fosters complacently. 'So I modified the studies before handing them over. As it turns out, in the wrong direction. Well, wrong in one sense anyway.'

The Pride looked at him carefully; he wasn't making much

sense. 'So you personally were pretty certain from the start that all these opinion polls we've had over the past six months have been erroneous?'

The Fosters laughed again. 'Look at it this way. If they hadn't been neck and neck do you think the Tories would have bothered to campaign so hard? What sort of force d'you think is needed, to make Cameron take off his jacket, roll up his sleeves and trail around the country, meeting real workers and yelling his slogans? It was the best way I could think of to shake 'em out of their comfort zone.'

'While all that time you knew their party was well ahead? Isn't that a bit unfair?'

'Hey, mate, it wasn't just the party. Think what would have happened if the media thought the Tories were going to win. They'd have torn their manifesto to shreds. I mean, it was only drafted as a starting point for discussion - that's the hidden benefit of Coalition. Election promises don't mean anything once you're tied in to rule with another party. The Tories never for a moment expected they'd have to implement it.'

'You mean, the press would just want to know where all the bribes would be coming from?'

'Probably. But with the polls level, they mostly kept asking instead about coalitions and secret deals and support on Confidence and Supply. Then the polls in Scotland gave a further twist. So the published polls skewed the whole election. Everyone – newspapers, columnists, readers, viewers - believed them.' He smiled. 'Everyone, that is, except me.'

This conversation was turning up far more insight than the Pride had expected. 'It's a pity you're an honest man. Or else you could have turned that to your advantage.'

'How d'you mean?'

'I reckon you'd get long odds – even yesterday – on there being a Conservative majority government at the end of this election.'

The Fosters nodded. 'Ladbrokes had odds of ten to one, as a matter of fact.' He shrugged. 'I put a hundred thousand on it.'

The Pride gulped and did a quick mental calculation. 'So by tomorrow morning you're likely to be a millionaire.' He gave him a careful look. 'But you don't look that pleased?'

'It didn't work out quite as I'd hoped,' admitted the Fosters. 'Trouble was, I told one of the campaign staff this evening what I'd done. It didn't go down too well. It seems the Tory High Command is not as keen on private enterprise as you might expect. I was sacked on the spot. So tomorrow morning I'm off to Ladbrokes to pick up my winnings, and then I'm catching a plane back to Australia.'

It was hard to think of anything more to ask; there was a lull in the conversation.

The Fosters finished his pint and prepared to battle to the bar for a refill. 'Can I get you another?'

'Better not. I need a clear head right now.'

An unexpected answer, prompting a further question. 'So what's your line?'

'I work for the Fraud Office,' said the Pride. 'We've a special unit looking at election scams. By all means have your drink. Then you and I need to go down to the police station and repeat our conversation in the interview room. You might not be on that plane after all.'

11. FOUNDRY FLOUNDERS

' And mind how you go, Mark,' Aunt Daisy admonished. 'Them roads is bad this time of year. With things as they are, the last thing we need is to lose our best marketer.'

I bit back a retort. "Only marketer" would be equally accurate. My uncle's wife was only ten years older than me but acted like the family matriarch. Given the state of the Sticklepath Foundry, I knew as well as she that we couldn't afford any more blunders. Hammers mislaid, hinge-rockers loosed from their hinges, machinery splintered: in every case production disrupted. Truth was, the amount of goods piled on the back of my wagon ready to sell – whether shovels or scythes, spades or pitchforks - had dropped steadily over the last few years.

It wasn't Daisy's fault, mind. It was all down to her husband; or to be more precise, to his toothache. I had some sympathy with Robert: it couldn't be much fun managing a foundry in a small Devon village with bad teeth – his own, I mean, not those of the villagers. 'So where was the dentist?' I hear you ask.

The truth was that in 1880 there were no dentists – at least, not in outlying parts of the country like ours. You see, Robert's toothache had started in 1869; and had got steadily worse.

It was two years after it began that he started to take laudanum. A casual visitor to the village, a drifter who had spent his early years as a soldier in the Crimean war and then fallen on hard times, sold Robert a small sample. He was to try it "first thing in the mornings".

And for a few days Robert seemed a changed man. Not only did it suppress the pain, but it lifted his spirits: he became fully human - almost cheerful. He took an interest in his foundry and how it might expand; even started to supervise the staff with some humility.

Then the laudanum ran out and he was worse than ever.

It was soon afterwards that I was asked to seek fresh supplies of the drug as part of my marketing duties. I took my goods round the county every month, see, so I was away most of the time. And Robert knew my tour always took me as far as Exeter. That was a big place, where a determined man could find almost anything. I didn't much like the idea but Robert was insistent – and desperate.

Discreet enquiries in Exeter market led me to a scruffy-looking man who operated out of a shack by the River Exe; and who had laudanum for sale – at a price. But whatever the price was, for Robert it would be worth it. And for the sake of his staff, if nothing else, I was prepared to pamper him.

So the routine was established. For many years the Foundry Manager became an intermittently happy man; while the income from my sales trips was increasingly reduced.

I say "increasingly" because the quantity of laudanum that I was asked to purchase rose steadily. Robert obviously enjoyed the drug for its own sake as well as for its impact on his toothache. Daisy told me once, almost in despair, that Robert had even become frisky around full moon. I didn't like the sound of that. It wasn't in my interest for a direct successor to the owner of the business to emerge. As his nephew I reckoned I was next in line.

Since the laudanum's price rose as well, there were greater and greater inroads into foundry income; and a matching reduction in our profits. By 1880, despite the strenuous effort of its workers, Sticklepath Foundry was struggling to break even.

I tried reducing the dose I brought back from Exeter; but Robert detected that. His staff spotted it as well: his bad temper recurred

65

sooner than usual after my homecoming - though they didn't understand why. From then on my uncle weighed the amount I brought him. 'I don't mind an excess, Mark,' he told me, 'but I won't tolerate a shortfall.'

After that I'd mixed the drug with similar, dark-coloured earth; but that hadn't worked either. I guess it affected the taste. At which point Robert examined the bundle carefully and spotted the dilution.

So for the last few months I had gone the other way: bought twice as much as I'd been told; and watched Robert become ecstatic - almost delirious - as a result. And the effect, month after month, was cumulative.

But I didn't mind. Flying as high as a kite meant there was no way he and Daisy could produce an heir. Which was fine: it left me as the only "next generation" now employed at the Foundry. The only question left in my mind was how much business there would be to inherit.

A month later I returned to Sticklepath. I'd sold all the foundry products I'd taken; and spent much of the resulting income on laudanum.

As I drew close I sensed trouble. Usually the Foundry was a cacophony of noise. The regular "ker-klunk, ker-klunk" of the water-powered forge press, pressuring red-hot iron into the shapes of shovels or scythes. The hammering of the special "fork 'andles" into the shovels and forks. And the acerbic aroma from the darkness - the smoke billowing out of the doorway from the furnace.

Today there was no smoke or smell; and no noise either. Whatever had happened? I hurried to the Foundry, leapt down and peered inside.

To find no-one there. This was Thursday - normally a hive of activity. Whatever had happened?

Stepping outside and looking up and down the street, I noted there was some activity – it was at the village chapel. What looked like a funeral service was about to begin. It was not too late to link to the mourners and I hastened to join them. As I'd been away, I didn't know who had died; but in our small village it was bound to be someone I knew.

And I did. As I slid into the chapel and eased into the backmost pew, my neighbour whispered, 'You won't have heard: we're here for Robert.'

The toothache's finally got him, I thought. It was a shock. I sat in a daze through the rest of the service. The chapel was gloomy, lit only by a few candles. Now I understood the occasion, it was no surprise to see Daisy, dressed in black, sitting alone on the front row. Poor girl; she'd not had much of a life. What would happen to her now?

There were refreshments for all of us back at the Foundry, once the service was over and Robert had been laid to rest. Poor chap; he was only in his mid-fifties.

I hastened to speak to Daisy as we wandered back – though she seemed to be eyeing me without much affection. I caught up with her beside the Foundry.

'This is a dreadful shock for us all,' I began, 'the toothache's finally got him.'

'Mark, let's not pretend. When Robert collapsed we had the doctor to find out what was the matter. He did some tests. It wasn't toothache – it was the laudanum. It's refined from opium, you know. The doctor checked; he had been taking extreme doses. Which, I believe, you supplied.'

I was shocked. Not by the doctor's diagnosis, but by the fact that Daisy had found out, somehow, that I was the source. I was about to challenge the whole notion when she continued, 'I heard you and Robert arguing over it many times. So don't you try and deny it.'

I had assumed Daisy would be stricken with grief but she

67

seemed oddly decisive. I had never thought of her anything more than Robert's domestic help-mate; but perhaps I was wrong. How could I broach the subject of taking over the Foundry, now that Robert was gone? Was it too soon, I mused, to be asking about his successor?

'In case you're wondering,' she went on, 'I'll be taking charge here now. And if you challenge me, I shall make sure the authorities are told you were the one supplying the laudanum. With some unpleasant consequences, I wager. I mean, to all intents and purposes, you killed him.'

I was flabbergasted. 'Hold on a minute. This is 1880. Women have no role in industry. They don't run companies – least of all in tiny villages.'

'They haven't up to now, Mark. But if Queen Victoria can run the Empire I think I can manage Sticklepath's Foundry. It's been in need of proper management for years.'

'But the Foundry will still need a marketer,' she continued. 'And if you'll accept me as boss then I'll keep employing you. But you'll find me a harder taskmaster than Robert. I may be only a woman but both my feet are firmly on the ground. And I'm as determined as any man to make this Foundry a success.

'Now,' she concluded, 'are we in this together, Mark – or will you be on your way?'

Finch's Foundry today is a National Trust site just off the A30 near Okehampton. Too near Cornwall to warrant a detour? No, it's well worth a visit.

12. MOLLY'S TALE

Reginald Rockall looked angry. He'd just taken a phone call from Mary Buchanan, an older lady whose war effort was to use her home for accommodating military personnel.

'Trouble?' asked his security boss, Simon Chandler-Hughes. The half of the phone conversation he'd overheard had sounded ominous.

'One of Mrs Buchanan's lodgers has disappeared, sir. Climbed down the drainpipe in the dead of night, she thinks. His room has been cleared, anyway. Damn, damn, damn.'

'Keep calm, Reg. What's his name?'

Rockall skimmed his notes. 'Stothard. Eamonn Stothard. One of the Park gardeners, she says. Or, at least, he was.'

Rapidly, Chandler-Hughes turned to the huge filing cabinet lining the wall, pulled out the relevant dossier and glanced through it. 'Hmm. He's been here since before the war, apparently. But he's only got basic site clearance. He wouldn't have access to any of the buildings.'

'Provided that stuff all works, sir. Who else is Mrs Buchanan supposed to look after?'

A second filing cabinet gave Chandler-Hughes the answer. 'Molly Filbert. She's one of our couriers. Does a regular weekly trip to the North of Scotland.'

'And is she still with Mrs Buchanan? Or has she bunked off with Stothard?' An unofficial liaison, while a technical breach of security, could be handled without wider ripples. They'd done it plenty of times before.

'Didn't you ask Buchanan about her other guests, Reg? Ring her back quick.'

A few minutes later another phone call was being reported. 'She says Filbert's always away on Wednesday and Thursday; left this morning after breakfast. But her room looks perfectly normal.'

'OK, Reg, we'll assume for the time being that she's innocent. But we'll have her in as soon as we can - find out what she might have given away.' He pulled a paper from the file. 'In the meantime, take this photograph and check the railway – see if anyone looking like him, with Park papers, took a train early this morning. And, if so, which direction they went.'

While Rockall was off at the station, Chandler-Hughes called in Jenkins, the Head of Maintenance and gave him the news that he was now a man short. Jenkins was sent back to question Stothard's late colleagues on any odd comments or behaviour. But Chandler-Hughes was not hopeful. This might just be a short-term absence. But it might also be the serious exposure of Bletchley Park which they had long feared.

An hour later Rockall was back with bad news. Stothard had been seen at the station just after six o'clock this morning – five hours ago. He'd caught the fast train to Birkenhead.

Chandler-Hughes consulted the railway timetable. 'Blast. Unless it's running late he'll already be there. Half an hour earlier, Reg, and our colleagues might have caught him at the barrier.'

Though Reg could do many things, making time run backwards was not within his brief. 'We can still send them the photograph, sir.'

'You're hopeful. By now, if Stothard's cunning, he won't look anything like his official photograph and he'll have false papers to match.'

'So the chances of him being caught now are close to zero.' Rockall looked despondent.

Chandler-Hughes was still aiming to be proactive. 'We need Molly Filbert back here as fast as possible,' he said. 'Go to the courier people, Reg, find out which army camp she'll be at next and tell 'em to send her straight back here. In the meantime I'll report what's happened to the Operational Commander.'

Molly Filbert was given no reason for the instruction, when she reached Catterick Camp, to return immediately to Bletchley Park; she was back just after two. She was told to report at once to the Security Office – she'd never been there before but it was obvious she was in some sort of trouble.

There had been strong disagreement between Chandler-Hughes and Rockall as to how to handle her. Rockall, who'd been badly injured, twenty odd years ago, on the Western Front, took a hostile view while his colleague, who'd been in charge of security at Cambridge University, wanted information rather than retribution.

It wasn't clear which approach would work best until the interview was underway.

'Sit down, please, Miss Filbert,' began Chandler-Hughes. 'We need to ask you some questions about Eamonn Stothard. I gather he shares a house with you?'

'Oh, is he alright, sir? He wasn't there at breakfast this morning.'

Chandler-Hughes did not reply. At a glance from his boss, Rockall took over the questioning. 'How well would you say you knew Stothard, Miss Filbert?'

'I've been in Bletchley nearly a year. For most of that time, despite sharing the same house, he and I hardly spoke. I wanted to keep to the security guidelines and Eamonn . . . well, he seemed shy. But in the last month we've started to become good friends.'

'Hmm. How good, Miss Filbert? Let's not hedge about here. I mean, are you sleeping together?'

Molly flushed. 'That's a very intimate question, sir.'

Rockall glowered. 'To which I want a direct answer.'

The girl was silent. This was not something she had ever expected to talk about – least of all to senior army officers. But they looked grim as they waited for her answer.

In the end she swallowed hard then made her confession.

'We slept together, sir, but only the once. That was last night.' She stopped but it was obvious, from the men's reactions, that much more was required. She took a deep breath to calm herself then continued.

'Mrs Buchanan – that's our landlady - announced at supper that she would be out for the evening. She said she was giving her next First Aid course down in the village. As soon as she'd gone, Eamonn turned to me, grabbed me by the hand and said this was our chance.'

'And of course you went along with him.'

'He was the one that was keen, sir. I – well, I'd never done it before but he seemed desperate. I . . . well, I suppose I felt sorry for him. I've been in this place so long, sir, I haven't seen my friends in ages.'

She turned to the senior man and asked again. 'Is Eamonn alright, sir?'

'How much have you told him about your duties?' asked Chandler-Hughes. He wasn't going to answer her question yet.

'For a long time nothing at all, sir. Then, a month ago, I had a nasty accident when I came home one night – skidded off the drive. He and Mrs Buchanan came out to see what had happened - between them they pulled me from under the motor bike and sorted me out. He was so kind to me, sir. I think I must have been in shock. I started talking; it slipped out that I had been up to Scotland. But I never told him exactly where, sir – or what I was carrying. Not that I know anyway.'

'So what else have you told him over the past month?' asked the senior man.

73

'Apart from my weekly courier trip, my job is to take parcels between buildings on the Park, sir. I've no idea what goes on inside. I mean, they don't have names, do they, just hut numbers. I told him bits and pieces about the people I handed over to – they were practically all women, of course. I made the odd comment about their home-made lipstick and so on. But I never said anything that you might possibly term secret. What has happened to Eamonn?'

Rockall glanced at Chandler-Hughes and received a slight nod. It was obvious to both men that Molly was not part of any espionage arrangement.

'Eamonn Stothard left Bletchley very early this morning, Miss Filbert. We believe he took a train to Liverpool. We fear he's on his way to Southern Ireland, to divulge whatever he's gleaned about the Park to the enemy.'

Molly looked completely stunned. For a moment there was silence in the small room. Then some of the pieces seemed to fall into place. Bitter recrimination started to replace her sadness.

'So the swine just had me as a last fling before he fled?'

'It would seem so,' replied Chandler-Hughes. 'That's why we need to understand from you everything – everything - he could possibly have learned about the Park before he left.'

Two hours later a shocked and exhausted Molly Filbert had been dismissed and sent to find food. Chandler-Hughes and Rockall pondered their next move.

'It seems unlikely, sir, that Stothard had access to any documents to take away with him. Miss Filbert didn't have anything to hand on. So whatever he might suspect, he couldn't prove what was going on.'

'No. He'd no clearance to go into any of the buildings - and we've no evidence that he did.'

'From all she told us, it seems Molly Filbert never gave him anything beyond tittle-tattle. A month of that is probably what drove him off.'

'Poor kid. She was pretty shaken up, Reg, don't you think?'

'What will happen to her, sir? Dismissal from the Park? Or – I know - a day in the stocks outside the canteen, under the banner, "She slept with the enemy"?'

As Rockall fulminated, Chandler-Hughes was looking again at Stothard's security file.

'Hm. That's interesting. I see it was you, Inspector Rockall, that checked Stothard in 1939 and gave him site clearance. Maybe it's you that needs a spell in the stocks?'

Rockall looked suitably abashed.

Chandler-Hughes, though, spotted something else in the papers. 'Hold on a minute. It says Stothard has been working here since 1938. That's before the Military even decided to take over the Park. So . . . it was just luck or clever guesswork that he happened to be here when the war started. It doesn't prove there's been any bigger leak.'

'So we might just get away with it, sir. If there are no air raids in the next month then it means he's not been believed.'

'Or else the Germans are so confident Enigma is invincible they can't believe there's a site set up in Britain to provide its decryption.'

The mansion at the centre of Bletchley Park, now a museum. The wooden huts used by the code-breakers are off to the right.

13. A WIG IS NO PROTECTION

Evan Jenkins had covered many things on his recently-completed medical course – but not facilitating resurrection. Right now it looked like that might be a serious omission.

For as he'd completed his early-morning mug of freshly-brewed coffee in the small cafe opposite the junction, a rather tubby-looking cyclist had come belting down the lane opposite, supposedly reserved for Olympic officialdom. It looked as if he had hit some sort of obstacle on the road. A smart, green Volvo, chasing behind him, screeched to a halt.

For a second Jenkins' vision was impaired. Then he saw him again. The man hadn't stopped, but had gone right across the traffic lights as they turned red; and, it seemed, straight under the front of the National Express coach, which was just starting to move forward in the opposite direction.

It looked as if he was the only one who had seen it all happen – or at least had observed the event and knew what to do. It was only six in the morning; there weren't many people about. Quickly he reached for his phone and dialled 999. 'I'm on the corner of Olympic Way and East Stratford Road – beside the Olympic Stadium. There's been a serious accident involving a cyclist. He went under a bus. We need an ambulance now, please.'

Then, remembering his Hippocratic oath, sworn just the month before, Jenkins hurried across the road to see what help he could offer.

One or two people were gathered round the now-stationary coach. There weren't any passengers on board. As he stepped forward he could see a head some way underneath – or at least, not the whole head, but a mop of unruly blond hair. The idiot hadn't even been wearing a crash helmet. Still, it wasn't the time to worry about that now.

Jenkins was not carrying a medical bag; he was on his way to register at Stratford Hospital. It was only because he had mis-judged the journey time from Caerphilly and arrived so early that he had stopped for a coffee. It was August 1st, his first day on duty; statistically the worst day of the year for patients as staff moved jobs throughout the NHS. The new pattern would take weeks to settle. But the cyclist wouldn't care about that – as long as he was still alive.

'I'm a doctor,' he told the observers standing around the bus, 'can I get to him, please?' He had been warned that London crowds were unfriendly, but that didn't seem to be true: they parted like the Red Sea when admonished by Moses.

He peeled off his smart, new jacket. Then, wishing it was anyone else but him on the front line – preferably someone who knew what they were doing and ideally were rather slimmer - he knelt down, lay flat on the road and started to wriggle under the coach. He couldn't yet hear any emergency sirens.

There wasn't much headroom; the bus was of Continental de-sign. He wasn't the slimmest of doctors – he played second row in his local rugby team - and could inch forward only slowly. It wouldn't help if he got stuck.

He was not far from the cyclist when he spotted a photogra-pher, peering under the far side of the bus. He was taking pictures – he wasn't sure if the focus of attention was him or the cyclist.

In theory Jenkins had always believed in freedom of the press but this was ridiculous. How the hell had the man got there so quickly? Why was he ahead of the ambulance? Was the cyclist someone of serious media interest?

'Oi - clear off, parasite,' Jenkins shouted. The tension in the whole scene made him unusually angry. 'Leave him alone - this is a matter of life and death.'

The photographer turned towards him, looking surprised.

It was a bulky piece of equipment he was holding; Jenkins realised to his horror that it was probably a video camera. It would record his less-than-kind words, as well as his almost-squashed body and his purple, furious face.

Then he remembered he was no longer just a student but a qualified doctor: image counted. The General Medical Council might not like the footage. It would be frustrating to be struck off before he'd dealt with his first patient.

But none of this mattered right now. He turned back towards the cyclist and struggled forward, intent on checking his condition. As far as he could see, the man wasn't moving.

Then he heard the sound of a siren. Thank goodness, an ambulance here at last. No doubt the paramedics would have more experience of traffic accidents than he had – and there was a good chance they would be slimmer.

Jenkins decided he really didn't need to be the first to the victim. Discretion was sometimes the better part of valour. He started to reverse direction. It turned out to be even harder to retreat than to go forwards: he wondered if he would require help to get out.

Whatever happened, he didn't want to be rescued by the ambulance team. It might get him to the hospital quicker, but it wasn't a good way to start his new job.

By the time he had backed out, looked around for his jacket, seized it back from a bystander - who looked to have been about to make off with it - and moved forward, much had happened at the front of the coach. While he had been struggling, the medical staff must have come forward with a stretcher then put the man into the ambulance. However it had happened, the cyclist was no longer under the bus.

To his annoyance Jenkins saw that the photographer was still filming events. By now he was accompanied by a woman, holding a notebook, who he assumed must be a senior reporter.

The young doctor strode forward to remonstrate then decided that a low profile would be better. He had been the one to call up the emergency services: that was enough.

Dusting himself down, he headed off for his first day in the hospital.

Two months later Evan Jenkins was shocked to be told by his new colleagues that he had been spotted acting in a new television safety campaign.

Eventually he found the programme, broadcast after the six o'clock news. It began with the junction where he had seen the accident. The plump, blond-haired cyclist appeared, followed by a smart car. The car braked hard as the lights turned red, but the cyclist slipped through. Next he was flying through the air and sliding under the coach.

After a pause an ambulance turned up, siren sounding; and the man was carried away.

Finally a healthy-looking Boris Johnson appeared, speaking earnestly about the need to wear cycle helmets and to take proper notice of traffic lights.

The campaign was broadcast regularly over the next month. As Jenkins saw it more often, he was able to spot himself in the background, sliding about under the bus. It certainly wasn't dignified. Mercifully, though, his abuse of the photographer had been blacked out.

14. PRIZE FOR PERSISTENCE

'So I came home one evening, just a couple of weeks ago, and she was gone.' Oddly, the speaker didn't look unduly concerned as he prepared to tackle his second Aspels.

'So who does yer washing now?' asked his drinking companion in the Copper Kettle, as he took another swig of Theakston's Peculiar and focussed in on the specifics that mattered.

'That's easy. Take it round to me sister every fortnight.' Handling the laundry obviously wasn't his main concern. 'Gwen was only living with me for a few months, see,' he went on. 'She was away more than she was home. Had some sort of decorating business, she told me – kept her out all hours.' He paused, brooding on his loss as he took a first sip of his cider.

He went on, 'It was just odd she didn't say goodbye. I was very fond of her - thought we had something special. Else I wouldn't have taken out the life insurance.'

'Not all bad news then,' his companion smiled.

'Well, it shouldn't have been. Two million quid she was insured for. You could do a lot with that – or more to the point, you wouldn't need to do much at all with all that behind you. "Jack," I told meself, "this is the end of your shelf-stacking." Trouble was,' he sighed, 'the insurance company wouldn't pay up.'

'That lot are almost as bad as bankers. What was their excuse?'

'They said there was no hard evidence that she was dead.'

Theakston's pondered for a moment. It was a casual encounter, he'd only just starting coming here – he had his own troubles at home - but was there anything he could say that might help Jack in

81

some way?

'Have you . . . have you been to the local hospital, say? Or the police?'

'What'd be the point? Half the cops are busy investigating high-level crime from the 1980s. Or else why they hadn't looked into it earlier. A few more are checking to see if someone from the papers had tapped their phones.

'She's not in the hospital, anyway,' he went on. 'She was only small but she was as fit as a fiddle. All I really need is a death certificate for Gwen that I can send to the insurers.'

'No, mate, what you really need is a woman's body that you could bury under Gwen's name.'

'Hmm, that's a thought. There's a Body Shop in the High Street . . .'

'No, I'm being serious. You've got all Gwen's paperwork at home – her birth certificate, passport and so on? If you were prepared to assert that a newly-found dead body of the right sort of height and age was your partner then you'd be away.'

His companion nodded slowly as he gave the idea some thought.

Theakston's went on, 'But we'd need some sort of deal before I helped you anymore. I'd need a share of that insurance, say, twenty five percent – I mean, I'd be the one taking most of the risk.'

The lately-abandoned man looked at him in surprise. Theakston's had mentioned being in a Writer's Circle; but apart from that he didn't know much about him. Was this a wind-up – or the start of his next writing assignment?

'Wait a minute - that's half a million quid. What sort of risk is needed to justify that much?'

'Unclaimed bodies aren't that easy to find, Jack. Not conveniently dead ones. But I've got a friend who boasts, when he's had a few, that he does "executions on demand". I think he's genuine. I could sound him out - if you were prepared to go through with it?'

The recently-bereft one was silent for a moment. 'I'd be alright as long as Gwen didn't reappear while we were busy arranging it. Why don't you make some enquiries? Meantime I'll phone round the friends that I know about. Do my best to make sure she's really dropped out of contact.'

The Theakston's Peculiar, Henry Grimthorpe, had a lot of thinking to do as he pottered home later. For, as it happened, he knew exactly what had befallen Gwen – or Wendy, as his wife Maria had known her. She was last seen lying drowning in a sea of slowly setting concrete beneath their slate kitchen floor. Although "seen" was not completely accurate. It had been pitch dark when he pushed her down into the depths: he was disappointed, later on, to find that it was not his wife that he had disposed of.

What a bizarre coincidence, then, to meet Gwen's late partner! Not that bizarre, maybe: there were only two pubs around here, so hardly a coincidence that two similar-aged men, both local, should be thrown together. He had a difficult marriage to keep out of, his companion no partner at all. But was this not a once-in-a-lifetime chance to complete the project that had gone so disastrously wrong – and dispose of his wife at a profit?

The trouble was, it would need meticulous planning – which, as his wife could testify, was not something for which he was well-known in the domestic arena.

Two nights later Henry and Jack met to complete their planning in the Copper Kettle.

'I got in touch with my friend, Sid,' said Henry, once they'd bought drinks and found a quiet corner. 'He took a bit of persuading but he'll do it for me as a parting gift for a hundred thousand. He's leaving for Australia next week so the timing's perfect.'

'And what about the . . .' Jack swallowed hard, 'the Gwen substitute?'

'For the rest of the money we were talking about on Tuesday, I'll supply the woman. That'll be my wife, Maria. We've been having difficulties lately; this is a painless alternative to a messy divorce. Painless for me, anyway. I think you said Gwen was small? Maria's not tall either so it'll be easy for you to pretend the body which you'll find in the bed used to belong to Gwen.'

'Er . . . what bed?' asked Jack nervously. 'I need to know what I'm paying for, see.'

'Well, let's assume Sid and I deal with Maria in our bedroom. I'm told careful smothering is almost undetectable so that's the easiest scenario for the death scene. I'll hold her still and he'll apply the pillow. After that we've got a choice.'

Henry took a sip of his Peculiar. 'There are two options. Either the two of us – that's Sid and I - carry her down the stairs and we move her body round to your house - put her into your bed, for you to find when you come in from the pub later. Trouble is, a body's not easy to move and it risks her being seen along the journey. Or else . . .'

'Or else what?' Jack frowned, his face puckering in alarm.

'You and I swap identities for a week. You'll come to my house when I call you, armed with all Gwen's paperwork. Then, once you've arrived and given me your keys, I'll slip round to your place. You can call the ambulance after you find her. Later on you can deal with the funeral people, the death certificate and so on. It'll be tough but you should have no problem afterwards with the insurance company. After all, you'll have a fully-dead body to claim on.'

Jack stared at him in horror. 'But . . . what if there are questions? Suppose – suppose, say, the ambulance men are suspicious and they call the police?'

'That's why you've got to spend that evening where you'll be seen – here, say. These days, doctors can call the time of death

84

pretty accurately - as long as it didn't happen ages ago. So they'll be able to prove "Gwen" died while you were here in the pub. You'd have the perfect alibi.'

Henry drew breath. 'Anyway, that's the worst case. It's more likely that an excessively-busy Health Service won't ask any questions at all. You'll just have to remember to keep referring to the dead woman as "Gwen" — oh, and of course to give them my address when you call them.'

Jack had other worries too. 'I don't much like this idea of us swapping identities and homes — even if it's only for a week. Someone will spot it, surely?'

'Well, let's think it through. Can I ask, do you get many personal visits?'

'The few friends I've got don't drop in uninvited, that's for sure. But both of us have got neighbours.'

'It's winter — no-one stops to chat. At the worst they'd just see us walking down the road. We're about the same height and build - how about if we swapped coats?'

'And we could each wear hats.' Jack was starting to warm to the idea. It was like a grown-up party game. 'That would deal with your hair being grey and me going bald. Folk 'd never notice.'

'And as for banks and utilities, nothing would change. A week of ignoring any letters that arrived wouldn't matter. It'd be just like each of us was on holiday.'

'Yeah. And if someone arrives, say, to read the meter, we'd let 'em do it. They're not going to remember us. We're just middle-aged blokes - virtually interchangeable.'

The pair talked for some time, going over difficulties and ways they could be overcome. Gradually the plan evolved from wishful daydream to hard reality. Maria's hours were numbered: her last day was fixed for one week's time.

Maria Grimthorpe had endured a dismal fortnight since her friend and lover had disappeared in her kitchen. Theoretically Wendy/Gwen might have been kidnapped by a burglar, but in her heart Maria knew she was under the slates - though since they'd been having an affair, she dare not admit that to her husband. He, too, was behaving oddly - out drinking more often. She could not imagine what was bothering him.

In the end the anxiety got to her and she contacted the police with her concerns. They had certainly not over-reacted.

'Do you have your friend's phone number? Well, leave her a message. We'll check back with you later.'

Maria had tried phoning but, of course, got no answer.

On the critical evening Henry showed no sign of going out. Amazingly he suggested - at half past eight - that they had an early night.

Maria was about to refuse then recalled that she was trying to make up for her infidelity so went along with his suggestion. She even agreed to liven up activities by putting on a blindfold, after changing into her flimsiest nightdress.

'I'm ready for you, Henry,' she called as she lay on her back waiting for him, snuggled under the duvet. Before long, she expected, the bedclothes would be thrown off and she would face the chill of the bedroom. She put her arms beside her, clenching fists ready for the impending shock. Ideas went through her mind on what Henry would do next.

It was doubtful, however, if any of her thoughts anticipated her husband kneeling astride her, gripping her tightly under the duvet and then holding down a large pillow over her head.

By the time she realised that this was not some special game he had just invented it was too late. Five minutes of steadily weakened struggle and protest gave way to a deathly silence. This time Henry had succeeded; Maria was dead.

Time for stage two. Henry spent a few minutes tidying the room; then seized his dead wife's phone and called Jack in the

Copper Kettle. 'It's all gone to plan. Come round as soon as you can.'

Ten minutes later his co-conspirator was knocking at the door.

'"Gwen" is upstairs. I'll show you. Now it's time for your part.'

The men climbed the stairs and Henry showed Jack the main bedroom. There was no need for words. Maria was lying at peace, face up, on one side of the bed. There was no sign of the struggle that had taken place earlier.

'I presume Sid's cleared off?' asked Jack.

'Yes, and he took the fatal pillow cover with him. Give me your keys; then I'll take your coat and be off to my second home. Give me five minutes, though, before you call the ambulance.'

Henry let himself out and strode down the road. As he did so a police car drove up and parked opposite.

Jack took a few minutes to familiarise himself with the Grimthorpes' house; he'd not been there before. Then, making sure he'd got the right address, he seized the phone and called the ambulance service.

Scarcely a moment later there was a hard knock at the door. That was quick, he thought.

But it wasn't the ambulance, it was a uniformed policeman.

'Good evening, sir. You must be Mr Grimthorpe?'

Jack gave an acquiescent nod.

The policeman continued, 'Your wife called us earlier today about her friend that went missing from here a couple of weeks ago – Wendy, her name was. I just wanted to check: was there any response to the phone call?'

Jack opened and shut his mouth but no sound came out. Eventually limited power of speech returned.

'Yes. But she's dead, officer, upstairs. Died in her sleep. I've just called the ambulance. I thought you must be them.'

Not the response he'd been expecting but the policeman had

87

been trained to be flexible. 'Can I see, sir? Being certain of death requires some training. It's possible the woman is still alive.'

Slowly, reluctantly, Jack led him upstairs and into the bedroom. The policeman knelt down beside the still woman and felt for her pulse. There was nothing.

'You're right, sir. I'm afraid she is dead.'

As he spoke there was a second knock at the door.

'That'll be the ambulance.' Jack rushed downstairs and opened the door, then led the crew upstairs. As they set up their kit, he and the policeman slipped downstairs into the kitchen to await news of their exertions.

'Just to be clear, sir, is the lady upstairs Maria or is it Gwen?' asked the policeman.

Jack tried to think clearly before he dared answer.

It was a pity that it was just at this moment Henry Grimthorpe, two streets away, decided to check all was well. Henry had left behind Jack's number when he'd swapped coats. So he tried to use the re-dial on Maria's phone to contact him. But he fumbled and it didn't work quite like he expected. It was Maria's most recent call that was repeated.

So it was that a mobile phone ring-tone could be heard from beneath the kitchen's slate floor.

The policeman had not come to the house looking for trouble. But he feared that all this would take some time to unravel.

15. CHALLENGES OF THE POLE POSITION

E gged on by her mum, Morwenna Trelawney had long wantec to be Queen in the Christmas festivities. The role meant sitting atop a Christmas tree as it was pulled on a float through the nar-row village streets and out to the end of the harbour jetty. There all the lights would be turned on and the float would be centre stage in the winter festivities.

As a teenager, downsides started to emerge. The Queen was dressed in a white tennis dress, not overly protected against winter wind and rain: it didn't look too warm. Usually December was overcast rather than stormy – though Morwenna recalled one year when the whole event was cancelled because of an impending storm. The Queen for that year had abdicated and the bun-fight to select her successor was delayed.

Morwenna was now a sixth former and commuted daily to Truro College with her friend, Alison Jenner. Alison, a leading light in college dramas, had been Queen the previous year. As the two girls travelled, Morwenna took the chance to learn more of the role's closely-guarded secrets.

'So how's the choice of Queen actually made?'

'Well, it's not a battle between the girls. The key factor is their dads – who's going to drive the tractor that pulls the float? For some reason, the dads all see that as a big prize. There's a massive haggle behind closed doors in the upstairs of the Wink.'

'So if I wanted to be Queen I'd need to get my dad enthused?'

'That's how I did it. It works best if dad and daughter are both keen.'

Morwenna could see a problem. 'Trouble is, my dad doesn't drive cars. He's mad on racing bikes, see. Out every Sunday whatever the weather. He's fit, mind - even wins the occasional race.'

'But can he drive?'

Morwenna shrugged. 'Dunno. My mum does all the driving.'

'Well, has she ever driven a tractor?'

'It can't be that hard. After all, it doesn't move very fast. The main problem would be climbing onto that high driving seat. She's not very big, my mum.'

Alison was thinking around other aspects. 'I don't think women have taken part in any previous haggling. It's time they were, mind. Tell you what, my dad's now part of the inner circle. I'll ask him when the crucial meeting is – and also about your mum.'

A week later, Alison reported back. 'The key meeting's at the Wink next Sunday. Half past eight. My dad says there's no reason why your mum can't come. As far as anyone else knows she could be standing in for your dad. Apparently the rules don't say anything about parental gender.'

Morwenna had been telling her mum about the forthcoming tussle. Annie Trelawney wanted her daughter Queen at any price. They could talk at length as her dad was out on his bike, training for a New Year race.

Sunday evening came. Annie Trelawney had watched Top Gear to find out what a petrol-head would wear but couldn't take Clarkson seriously – there were no women on the programme at all. In the end she decided to dress as if for a party. Her husband was out cycling so was not in a position to comment - though he might have raised his eyebrows at the slinky, low-cut dress she had chosen.

It was not far to the Wink. Annie could hardly have made more impact if she'd turned up in a bikini. She'd never been the only woman at a man's party and revelled in the attention. She knew most of the men – it was, after all, only a small village – and Alison's dad, Geoff Jenner, was expecting her. He chatted to her as drinks were circulated. She had planned to stay clear of alcohol for the evening but found there was no alternative.

By the time the business part of the evening began her head was starting to spin.

'There are one or two newcomers this evening,' began the convenor, smiling broadly at Annie. 'I'll outline our procedure.

'The aim of this evening,' he went on, 'is to choose the family to lead the Christmas celebration. By that I mean one person to drive the tractor and trailer round the village, and a second – I guess a lady - to act as the Queen on the Christmas tree.'

OK so far, thought Annie.

'Anyone can bid; and the winner's cash – less 10% for our running expenses – will go to last year's driver. The highest bid will be determined by auction and I'll act as the auctioneer.'

Annie had known funds would be needed. The Trelawney's were not wealthy, but they had recently had a windfall. Her husband had won £250 on a West Country road race and, without prompting, had handed the winning cheque over.

'Some compensation for all the times I've been out training.'

Annie had not argued. As soon as she could, she'd converted the cheque into cash. She wasn't planning to bid it all but it was a useful reserve.

The bidding began. The opening bids were just a few pounds. Slowly the sums rose.

'£45.'

'Thank you,' said the auctioneer. 'Any advance on that, lady and gentlemen?'

Her time had come. '£50,' said Annie, raising her hand to make sure she was seen.

'£60,' responded a man behind her.

For a moment there was silence. The auctioneer raised his

gavel.

'£70,' said Annie. More than she'd planned, but she knew how much her daughter wanted to be Queen.

'£80,' came the voice from the back. Was it polite, Annie wondered, to turn and stare at her rival; or was it best to stay facing the auctioneer?

'£90,' she said.

Once again the back-of-room voice outbid her. The winner was going to be her or him. Without that third glass of Chardonnay, Annie might have capitulated; but now her blood was up. She had funds and if necessary she would spend them.

Steadily the bidding rose.

'£240,' said the man at the back.

'£250,' responded Annie. She tried to make sure that there was no change in her posture but she knew this was her last effort. Her tense body told the rest of the room as well.

There was an agonising silence. Then the auctioneer banged his gavel. 'Gone for £250.' A spontaneous round of applause: all the men around her gave Annie a hug. Morwenna would have her turn at being Queen.

On next morning's school bus Alison looked very embarrassed. 'Your mum went way over the top.'

Her mum had told Morwenna she was to be the next Queen but had not disclosed any details. 'How much did she pay?'

Alison had had the whole tale from her dad. 'You really don't want to know. One of the men – Barney Wilson - had decided he didn't like a woman taking part; he pushed her to the limit.'

Morwenna was horrified. 'Oh, no. I didn't want my mum humiliated. I mean, it's only a bit of fun. When I was young it seemed so special but . . .'

'It's not that much fun, actually. You have to pretend it's great so another girl wants to do it next year. I took it as an exercise in acting. It'd be good practice for performing at the Minack Theatre. Weather's never an obstacle down there.'

'OK, Alison, I can see you'll be very cold. But I've been cold before – playing hockey, for example. What else is so difficult?'

'Well, for one thing, once you've reached the jetty you can't go to the loo - for a couple of hours. So I trained myself beforehand – never went when I wanted to, forced myself to hang on for an hour every time.'

'Ouch.' It sounded uncomfortable.

'Of course, you have to keep pretending to smile even as you grit your teeth.'

Morwenna was starting to have serious doubts. 'Is that all?'

'If there's much wind – as there often is - you feel as though you'll be blown off the pole – or else that the thing will keel over and dump you over the edge. I didn't fancy a dip at that time of night – not without a winter wetsuit, anyway.'

The whole thing sounded dire. 'OK, Alison, you've convinced me. You are my witness. Even if they beg me, I will never be Queen. The question is, how can I avoid it?'

In the end it was Morwenna's dad who found a way out. He was best mates with Barney Wilson and cornered him that evening in the Wink.

'What if you'd won the auction?' he demanded. 'You haven't even got a daughter.'

'I was pretty sure I wouldn't win. Your wife's bidding strategy was very easy to read. If it had all gone wrong, I suppose I'd have had to take my wife. She would have hated it.'

'Well, how about this for an idea, Barney? We'll split the cost of the bid - then you can drive the tractor and my wife can go as Queen. Morwenna's told me she simply won't do it – I think her mum was the motivating force anyway.'

So that December it was Annie Trelawney who took her place

93

on top of the Christmas tree, as the float wended its way round the streets and out on to the jetty. As she shivered and wobbled about in her daughter's tennis dress in the bitter cold she could see why none of the girls – least of all Morwenna – had wanted the role. And why no-one ever did it twice.

There was a more hostile campaign, Annie thought, needing to be waged in the village next year.

*A Cornish harbour in mid-summer sunshine. Both jetties crammed with car-park overflows. The first Cornish Conundrum, "**Doom Watch**", starts in the harbour-town of Padstow.*

16. SMALLNOSE TAKES HIS REVENGE

There was an ear-splitting scraping noise on the window, followed a few seconds later by a skidding noise, a dull thud and then a muttered curse.

'What the blazes was that?' hissed a voice further back.

'There was something very slimy on that window ledge. I lost my grip,' came the whispered reply. 'Ouch - I've really twisted my ankle.'

'You'll lose more than your grip if you're not careful. Remember the instruction: we mustn't turn on the lights or make a noise and we shouldn't leave any trace behind. Now, assuming you counted the windows along properly, and we've actually managed to find his study, where do you think he might have hidden his desk?'

The two men were dressed in dark boiler suits, their faces covered with black balaclavas; they each wore thin nylon gloves. But despite their professional appearance they were not experienced burglars: Sam's explosive entrance had stretched their nerves to breaking point. At least the more senior, Albert, had remembered to bring a torch. This he started to pan slowly around the room.

They were not in the Einstein league of burglars, but it didn't take them long to conclude that they weren't in a study. They would argue, much later, about what had gone wrong with their counting: Albert maintaining that they had missed out the alcove port-hole, while Sam retorted that 'counting from the right' probably meant their right rather than the house's.

But for the moment there was relief when the beam latched on to an open doorway, leading through to what could well be a

95

study.

The pair crept silently forward and into the veterinary surgeon's private den.

They had reached the pet specialist's desk and had just started to go through the drawers when a voice from the far side of the darkened room made their hair rise and their blood curdle.

'You'll pay for this one day.'

Both burglars froze. Before they'd even found the damning, maltreated horse photographs they had been sent to retrieve, they had been spotted. There was a few seconds total silence, during which the two computed the chance of finding their way out before they were captured; and decided that they were nil.

'He told me you were coming,' the mystery voice continued. 'Hurry up, please, I need the loo.'

Slowly Albert turned his torch from the depths of the desk drawer and across the room. And there it came to rest on a large, green parrot, in a small cage, peering at them with some interest. The bird blinked as the beam caught him square in one of his beady eyes, coughed abrasively and said, sharply, 'Turn that bloody thing off.'

Shaken as he was, Albert was quick to obey.

In the resulting gloom Sam said, 'Do you remember, they said Mr Smallnose had some unusual security arrangements. Do you reckon they meant the parrot? And if so, was that all they meant?'

Being scared of a parrot was ridiculous, thought Albert. If the word ever got out into the villain community, they'd never live it down. But before he had time to articulate this thought, he felt something slithering over his canvas shoes. He froze again: what the hell was that?

Keeping still was obviously the best response. At least he assumed that was why whatever it was had left him and gone on towards Sam, who was shuffling slowly between the birdcage and the curtained window, exercising his twisted ankle. Albert guessed that was where the creature had reached from the terrified gasp and muffled scream issuing from his colleague, even before he'd shone the torch.

To be sure, it wasn't a big snake. He'd seen a much bigger one – was it a boa constrictor? - on Attenborough's TV programmes from Indonesia. But it didn't look like a harmless grass snake either: it certainly had a vicious bite. He gathered that much from Sam's gasp of pain as the reptile raised its elegantly patterned head, inspected his boiler suit then stuck its fangs through the cloth and into his calf.

'That's done it.' Albert realised with a shudder that it was the parrot speaking. Maybe it was used to the snake's share of the operation: a regular pincer movement.

It came to Albert in a flash that he and Sam hadn't been the first choice burglars for this operation. He remembered being surprised when they had been chosen. Now he perceived that more experienced pairs had been here before them - and had suffered similar fates. Maybe, if he could find one of their predecessors, he would learn more details about the snake?

For example, was its bite meant to paralyse or simply to kill?

But that would take days. Sam had already collapsed on the floor and was shuddering in pain: he needed to be taken to a hospital quickly.

Then he remembered one more observation from Attenborough: snakes weren't like bees, with just one sting. This one could easily bite again. How might it be distracted? A moment of inspiration struck him – the parrot.

Silently Albert crept across the room, unhooked the bird's cage from its frame, opened the door and set it on the floor. For a second he feared that the bird would simply escape, but for the moment it was too absorbed by the change of view – it had never seen right under the desk before. 'Get this lot cleaned quickly,' it squawked.

Albert could have advised the parrot that silence was the best policy. But now it was too late. The snake had enjoyed his starter bite of Sam but now there was something even more tasty in view – and it was a more interesting colour and of a more manageable size. The reptile quickly slithered over to the cage, lifted his head up to the open doorway and, with an elegant shuffle, pulled himself inside.

Albert might not be the brightest patch on the paint-chart, but he could see that this was his chance. Swiftly he reached over, shut the cage door, clipped the catch and locked the snake inside.

Examining it, he saw with relief that it was a well-constructed cage and the wires which enclosed it were placed close together. Without several days' strict diet, the snake would struggle to wriggle between them. The hostile reptile was stuck with the talkative parrot for the immediate future. The two creatures were eyeing one another with some curiosity.

But for now Albert could turn his attention to Sam. 'I'd better get you to hospital, mate. If I support your weaker side, can you stagger as far as the car?'

He could - just. It was as well the car was parked right outside the window where they had entered. Measured by a clock, that was not long before: now it seemed like a lifetime.

Retracing their path through the window was particularly tricky, but their motivation was strong. They didn't know what other fearsome creatures the vicious vet might have left loose in the surgery. Eventually Sam was outside and slumped inside the vehicle.

'To get the right antidote, won't they want to know what sort of snake it was?' the injured man asked, through clenched teeth.

'We can do better than that,' replied Albert. He got out of the car and clambered once more through the window. A few minutes later he re-emerged with the parrot's cage dangling from his hand.

'I suppose your idea is they'll ask the parrot and he'll say what it was,' muttered Sam. 'He seemed to know more about what was going on than we did.'

'Numskull. I've got the snake in here along with the parrot. The hospital doctors can take a look at it and work it out for themselves. If the worst comes to the worst they can look it up via Google.'

It was a bad evening, thought Sam, when his future existence depended on a search engine.

'Well, even so, I'm not driving anywhere with that pair in the back seat: no doubt the bird will have some salty comments on your driving.'

'OK, if you insist, we'll cover the cage so they can't see what's going on. Where's our swag bag?'

The burglars routinely carried a pair of dark-red old pillow cases with them to protect any valuables they found on their expeditions. They were virtually unused. With a bit of effort Albert found one which could just be fitted over the cage. He tied a piece of string round the top to secure the cover then took his seat behind the wheel.

'I'll need to hurry. We don't know how long we've got before the poison's reached too far.'

'Never too late,' croaked the parrot optimistically from behind his curtain.

Sam wasn't so sure. He could feel the bitten calf stiffening up and the absence of feeling inch slowly up his injured leg. Further up his body he felt faint and nauseous. 'Hurry up, please,' he pleaded, 'I don't think I've got long to live.'

Albert drove as fast as he dare. It was a good job it was dead of night and there was no other traffic. If it had been able to see, no doubt the parrot would have criticised the way he jumped the lights. Fortunately he knew the location of the main hospital. Once they reached the Accident and Emergency entrance he abandoned the car (it was stolen anyway) and helped his half-collapsed companion to the reception desk.

'He's suffering from a deadly snake bite,' he explained.

'You really don't need face masks in here,' observed the staff nurse. With some embarrassment Albert removed his and his companion's balaclavas.

A further thought caused him to peel off their gloves. He didn't want to round off the evening by being mistaken for a surgeon.

As Sam had predicted, the doctor who was called needed to know the type of snake. Albert slipped back to the car and returned with the covered cage. 'It's in here,' he explained. 'I managed to capture it.'

It was sounding odder and odder, thought the nurse. She resolved to call the police once the immediate crisis was over.

The doctor struggled to untie the knot and slide down the cage's cover. He had no idea it had been a bird cage until its recent transformation.

But Albert did; he spotted the parrot's small mirror as it came into view. Sadly, the beautiful parrot was looking into it no longer. The snake had seized his chance to move onto his main course.

Unprovoked killing, thought Albert. Though his burgling partner was not so sure.

17. CAUGHT ON THE REBOUND

I admit it: it was my fault.

It was my first morning, see; I rushed at the entrance door just as someone, racing almost as fast, came the other way and pulled it open. The end result was that I fell into his arms and the two of us landed in a messy heap on the floor.

Fortunately there was no-one else there – they'd all had the wisdom to come to the induction in good time.

'Are you all right?' he asked as he helped me up. 'My name's Jim – Jim Salting. I'm new here.' I saw a tall man in his late twenties with piercing blue eyes, fair tousled hair and a cheerful grin.

I laughed and held out my hand. 'I've been knocked about before, Jim. I'm Lauren – Lauren Shaw. This is my first day in police uniform. My mum told me to watch out, but I had hoped to get inside the door before the beatings started.'

This was Scarborough, 2007. Race relations were brittle in some parts of the country but there weren't enough West Indians to disturb life here. I'd grown up in the town and been glad to apply for a job in the police - hadn't realised, then, the tensions I'd encounter.

In the coming weeks Jim and I were new kids on the block together, which was perhaps why we bonded so well. Turned out he'd just made Inspector and come north from cosmopolitan London. Jim was used to West Indians and could tease me without giving offence. The local Officers were more stuffy and harder to win over.

It was perhaps because he'd started to know me – and liked

101

what he saw - that Jim gave me a chance to show some initiative. 'I'd like a quiet chat, somewhere out of the way – where d'you suggest?' he asked, as I passed his canteen table on my way off duty.

'The cafe in Peasholme Park, five thirty,' I whispered back. 'D'you want me in uniform or dressed for a dance?'

'The dance, of course. But don't tell anyone.'

This sounded interesting. So far I'd been little more than a high-grade traffic warden. Television's "Prime Suspect", Jane Tennyson, had far more dramas than I did – hers, mind, were in London.

I was in the Park early – I'd learned something by now about punctuality. Jim was already there, he'd found a quiet table at the back. 'Tea or coffee?'

'Black coffee,' I replied. 'They make it taste good here.'

'I'm trying to set up an undercover operation,' Jim began. 'But I'm finding it very hard to get high level backing.'

It'd never occurred to me that a white man might meet prejudice too. But this was Yorkshire and Jim came from the south. Maybe he was just as much an outsider as I was?

'I'm keen to make a difference if I can, Jim,' I replied. Despite the difference in rank we'd been on first name terms since that opening dust-up - I only called him "sir" in the office. 'What's it all about?'

'I had word from my old mates in London. They said they'd picked up rumours about someone here, who'd got a taste for underage girls.'

Puzzling. But it didn't ring any bells: I would need to know more. 'How young?'

'Not small kids, I think. Just young teenagers – mostly girls, growing up too fast for their own good. And dazzled, perhaps, by a high profile.'

I looked at him carefully. 'Can you tell me more?'

'The rumours were about some cricketer called Aaron

102

Schofield.'

'It can't be Aaron,' was my first response. 'I mean, he's the local legend. Would have been Yorkshire's greatest batsman since Geoffrey Boycott, so they say, if he hadn't gone and lost his arm in a boating accident.'

'Lauren, do you know him?' Jim seemed excited.

'Not personally. But he did prize-giving at my school one year. And caused half the girls to swoon. His face wasn't messed up by the accident, you see; he'd be quite a catch.'

Jim looked like he was grappling with a variant of a strange religion. 'Aaron's not so well-known down south, I'm afraid.'

'He may be unknown outside Scarborough, Jim, but here he's the local hero - the big after-dinner speaker. And he still does cricket coaching for youngsters once a week, in that big sports hall next to the Ayckbourn Theatre. Anyone can attend – even my young sister goes sometimes. The courses are very popular.'

'I'm sure they are.' In Yorkshire, Jim knew, cricket was a matter of life or death, not just a recreation.

I remembered we weren't here to discuss cricket. 'So what d'you want me to do?'

'I fear my bosses have been dazzled by celebrity too. They'd rather not do anything. But before I tackle that I need to know for myself if there's anything in the rumour.'

'You need hard evidence.' I'd learned that in my training: whispers didn't count.

'Yes.' Jim was silent for a moment, weighing up options.

'Ideally what I'd like would be for someone young and pretty to put themselves in Aaron's ambit. Someone who looked like they might only be 14 or 15. I'd watch carefully and see what he did.'

I didn't bother to evaluate the risks: this was the chance for action. 'Jim, My mum always said I looked young for my age. I can never buy alcohol without hauling out my driving license: they all think I'm fifteen. I could do it - if you think I'm pretty enough, that

103

is. When do we start?'

Enquiries showed the coaching sessions were still happening and took place on Sunday evenings.

The next Sunday afternoon I delved in my wardrobe and found items I should have thrown away years ago - but which might aid the deception. I'd still got my trainers, some tight-fitting white jeans and a body-hugging blue top that emphasised my almost-boyish figure. Finally I took out all the clips and let my hair hang loose. Once again, after a break of five years, I felt like a tearaway teenager.

There was no problem gaining access to the sports hall. I just had to sign in and hand over a quid. There were about twenty five kids there, mostly younger than me – some even younger than I was pretending. It was the start of the summer holidays but I guess these were mostly poor kids that wouldn't be going anywhere. My sister was there, too, but as usual we ignored one another.

Aaron Schofield was in charge, with a couple of assistants. He split the kids into groups and then rotated us around batting, bowling and fielding, with a mop-up session on fitness. I'd been OK at sport at school and was fitter than most of the regulars. After a couple of hours hard work we made our way to the bar and cafe upstairs.

I needed something cold. I pushed to the bar, close to the end where Aaron had perched himself, and ordered a lemonade. I'd have preferred cider but, I reminded myself, I wasn't supposed to be old enough.

'Not seen you here before,' I heard the coach comment.

I turned to face him. 'I'm new in Scarborough – here for a holiday job. You taught us well.'

'You're here on your own?' Aaron looked surprised.

'That's right. I'm staying with an aunt.'

'An aunt?' he asked cautiously.

'Well, a sort of aunt. She's not too fussed what I call her as long as I pay some rent.'

'And what's your name?'

'Lauren. And you're Mr Schofield. I know you; I've seen your pictures in the paper.'

It was good to be known as famous – and would make his largesse seem more acceptable.

There was a short delay while he processed options. Then, 'Lauren,' he asked, casually, 'how would you like to see a bit more of Scarborough?'

'Tonight? Bit late, isn't it?'

'Not if you've got the right key. We've been here for hours - it's time to move on. Why don't we go now?'

He held open a rear door. I hoped the monitoring gadgets were working on my phone. We walked down a narrow passage and out into the street.

Did he plan to use a car? How wide had Jim spread his listening net? I didn't want to find myself abandoned on the moors.

No, Aaron didn't need a vehicle. He led me, rapidly, through back streets, steadily gaining height.

'Where are we going?' I puffed, trying to keep up. He was tall and had a long stride.

'Home,' he replied. 'And you know, Lauren, an Englishman's home is his castle.'

'I'm sorry, Mr Schofield, I don't understand?'

But he didn't need to say more. For at that moment we came round a corner. Above, brightly floodlit, were the brown-granite walls of Scarborough Castle. You probably know it - the Castle stands proud on the headland that separates the north and south bays. It's a famous Yorkshire landmark. Was it here that he needed the special key? And if so, what did he plan to do once we were inside?

It wasn't too late, I thought. I could make a run for it. I doubted he would give chase: he wasn't that fit. But he hadn't yet said anything conclusive. The words recorded on my device had no strong proof of wrongdoing. Jim would still be left with rumours.

It occurred to me, too late, that I hadn't properly thought this project through: the cost might be very high. It was with some trepidation I let him take my arm then lead me up to the entry gate.

Six months later I was called to the Sessions in York. The arrest of Schofield had been a local sensation and attracted national attention; now was time to see what the Courts made of it.

The prosecution counsel first led me through the events at the bar. A transcript (from my recorder) had already been lodged as evidence. The words were not in dispute but were open to interpretation.

'So what happened, Ms Shaw, once you were inside the Castle?'

'Mr Schofield led me through the ruins. It was fairly dark – the floodlights were for outside - but he seemed to know where he was going. He guided me down some steps to a sort of dungeon - which was really dark. Now I was scared. I kept asking him what we were doing but he wouldn't answer.'

'I see. What happened next?'

'He asked me if I'd had ever had full-blown sex. I told him I hadn't. Then he asked me how old I was. I said I was just fifteen.'

'And how did Mr Schofield respond?'

'I heard him rub his hands. Then he told me that it was always good if a girl's first experience of sex was with a man who'd had plenty of practice – a man like him. I feared what was coming next, so I felt in my pocket for my phone and pressed the panic button.'

'And then?'

'Inspector Salting, my boss, must have been very close outside. He raced in, holding a big torch; then he shouted "You're under arrest" and slipped handcuffs on Mr Schofield. He gave him a full police caution. But Mr Schofield didn't say anything.'

Soon it was time for defence counsel to cross-examine. I'd been warned this would be tough. There was one matter uppermost in his mind.

'Ms Shaw, how old are you?'

'Twenty. I'll be twenty one next month.'

'So why did you tell Mr Schofield you were "just fifteen"?'

'That was what I'd agreed with Inspector Salting.'

'I see.'

Slowly the defence counsel turned towards the judge.

'Milord, This is a clear case of police entrapment. This witness was a Police Officer in disguise. She came dressed like a fifteen-year old and then lied about her age to arouse the accused's attention. Consenting sex between adults may or may not be sensible but is not a criminal matter. Surely, I contend, the accused has no case to answer?'

The judge was also disturbed. 'The case is adjourned until this matter has been determined. Clear the courtroom. Both counsels will see me in my room immediately.'

'So like many public figures, the swine has got away with it.' Jim was holding a case review, a week after the trial had collapsed.

'Perhaps we picked him up too early, sir?'

'You mean, I should have waited till he'd satisfied his lust?' Jim was bitter. Exercising duty of care for his colleague had led to justice being thwarted. And he'd been given no benefit of the doubt. Despite his endeavours his stock had sunk with higher authority.

'Or we could try again, using my sister.'

'You what?' Jim looked like he might explode. I hastened to explain.

'There were plenty of youngsters there, sir. Lots of choice for Schofield. He didn't pick me because I was the prettiest.'

'No?' Jim hadn't considered this angle.

'No. I reckon he picked me as I was one of the few that he hadn't been with already.'

'What on earth makes you think that?'

'Inside information, sir, from my sister. The coverage on the trial brought Schofield's predilections to light. Up to that point, though many had suffered under him, they'd each kept it to themselves. Felt ashamed, I suppose.'

Jim nodded. I continued, 'But the trial changed all that. They all hoped, of course, that it would do for Schofield. After it collapsed they started talking to one another. And once they saw my name as a witness, they started talking to my sister. I had a letter from her this morning, giving me a list of all the ones that have spoken to her.'

I reached inside my jacket and handed over a list of names and addresses.

'D'you think, sir, we'd have a better chance next time if the prosecution were to call in all this lot?'

18. A PAINFUL FILLING

The trouble all began with the "burglary that never was". That was what my master called it, anyway.

He and the wife had been away over Easter, you see, and I'd had the house to myself. Then the aspiring burglars came, heaving at the front door, smashing the glass window at the top and putting their grubby, gloved hands through the broken pane. I was in the hall and one of them saw me through the letter box. He gave a shout - of triumph, I presume - and I feared that I would be the first of their trophies.

But for some reason, despite giving it a good kick, they couldn't get the front door open.

I heard them go round the back and try the French windows. They'd have got in that way – they're pretty old, are those windows, designed before they'd invented burglars – but I heard shouts from next door, then the villains scarpered.

I presume the neighbours must have called my master home; he came the same evening. I could see he was cross. He should have been pleased: I mean, I was still in my place; and surely I was their most valued possession? And his wife – well, his wife was paranoid. She couldn't have been more incensed if they'd come home to find the house had been burnt to a shell.

She gave my master hell. 'I told you this place wasn't safe. We need new French windows – ones that lock properly. They've got some fashionable ones in that garden centre down the road; I've fancied them for years. And in the meantime you'd better get a second lock on that front door.'

109

In vain did the poor man plead that the front door hadn't been breached; that he was a dentist, for pity's sake, not a latter-day Mr Fixit. He went on to explain that he didn't have all the tools he would need.

The trouble was, with the burglary having failed, it wasn't even as though there was insurance money he could use to fund the extra items needed – let alone to buy new French windows.

But he had no chance: his wife was in no mood for logical debate.

The next morning the pair of them were off to B&Q, to buy a new door lock. My master announced that if he had to become a joiner for the day, his wife would be the joiner's mate. I heard them drive ferociously down the drive; then, a couple of hours later, and apparently reconciled, they were back.

They had bought the strongest mortise lock in the store. I heard him read out the notice on the cover: 'fit-able in a few minutes'. Even I, with no experience of fitting anything, could see that was unlikely to be true.

Not by my dentist-doorman, anyway.

There was already an old lock on the front door; but they'd never been given the key. So their first task was to take this out. The husband was just about up to undoing the screws. Once this was done, his helpmate's brute force took over. She was a strong woman.

Within half an hour the old lock was lying on the hall table. We could see it was a lot smaller than the new one they'd bought to replace it.

'That's inflation for you,' asserted the wife.

'More like evolution,' my dentist replied. 'Humans have got bigger over time: so have door-locks.'

Whatever the reason, they would need to enlarge the hole in the door before the new lock would fit where the old one had nestled.

At this point life started to get interesting. For although neither of my owners had any training in woodwork, the attempted burglary had fired them up and they were ready for the challenge. Though, to be fair, they were starting from a long way back.

The wife sometimes referred to me as a 'waste of space', but as far as I could see, the only practical skill which they had acquired in their fifty years on the planet was dentistry.

'How do you reckon we should make that hole bigger?' asked the dentist, as he peered at the four-inch hollow in the edge of the door.

'How about a chisel and mallet? I saw them in the garage only last year.'

Half an hour's search later, a chisel was found; but it proved too wide to access the gap in the door.

'Any more ideas?' asked the dentist.

'How would you operate if this was a patient's tooth?'

'Oh, that'd be easy,' he replied. 'I'd just apply my dentist's drill. Hey – wait a minute.' And he rushed off once more to the garage.

He'd not used it for some years, but he did own a Black and Decker power drill; and yes, it did still work.

But the problem wasn't completely solved. For even if in some pain, the dentist's patients would remain fairly still while their teeth were being drilled and re-filled. Whereas the inanimate front door, with its well-oiled hinges, had no such sense of stoic discipline.

The dentist had assumed that his wife could provide the re-straining force as he drilled. But after she had twice failed to resist his advance, the second time only just missing being gruesomely impaled on the door by the drill, she refused to continue.

'It must be possible to wedge it,' she pleaded.

A collection of magazines was gathered from the dentist's surgery and the best one for width was chosen to wedge the door in place. Now, with a passive target - his wife standing well aside - my master redoubled his efforts.

'Can I make a suggestion?' asked the wife after some time, when the trainer joiner seemed to be wilting.

'Yes?'

'When you operate on your patients, do you work in the dark?'

'Course I don't; I've got an adjustable spotlight that I position overhead.'

'Well, if we got that desk lamp from your study, we could point it into the gap in the edge of the door. Then you could see which corner you needed to work on.'

'Brilliant.'

The bond of common purpose brought them closer than I had seen for years. This was truly therapeutic – maybe even a rekindling of their marriage. A few moments later the desk lamp was arranged in the hall, pointing at the edge of the door.

'Do you want to have a go?' asked the dentist magnanimously.

I felt so proud of him. His wife had waited thirty years for this invitation. She did not hesitate. She stepped forward with the power drill and concentrated on the top right corner, which was rougher than the rest. This was an ideal task for her to start with - it required enthusiasm rather than experience and skill.

Soon the awkward corner was gouged close to perfection.

'Shall we try the new lock now?' she asked.

Of course, it did not fit; but it was not far off. Half an hour's more scraping and drilling, accompanied by cheerful banging and swearing, and it sank neatly into the door. Cheers on all sides.

'We'd better make sure the door still shuts,' suggested the wife.

But, sadly, the lock had not been sunk quite far enough into the door.

'So in the last two hours we've replaced a door fitted with a lock and no key – but which closed - with one with a solid lock, that won't close at all,' observed the dentist. He wasn't sure whether to laugh or cry.

'All we need is a wooden hammer to knock it in a fraction fur-ther,' said the wife.

It was a pity, I thought, that the search for a wooden mallet earlier on had been so unfruitful. That would have been ideal.

The wife looked around the hall; then her eyes seemed to fall on me. 'There's that dark, wooden African statuette of yours. I've never liked it. It'd be perfect for hammering that lock in.'

I could sense that my master was not happy with the suggestion. But he was never one to stand up to his wife when she was in full flow. I hardly need to say that I was speechless.

A few seconds later I had been seized by the base then cracked down, head first, onto the new lock. I had often wondered what happened when the irresistible force met the immoveable object. The answer, it turned out, was a lot of pain. But a wooden statuette like me never had a chance against a metal lock – one chosen, after all, as being the most secure in B&Q.

The lock was eventually manoeuvred into place and served the master and his wife for years. I was retired back to my shelf in the hall, head badly dented. I never recovered the polished charisma of my earlier years.

I sometimes wonder if it would have been better - for me - if the burglary had succeeded. I might have won the hearts of the burglars; they might have liked African artwork.

On the other hand, I might have ended up as their battering ram, used to club my way through a series of doorways and windows. Being seen and not heard is perhaps, after all, a more welcome accolade.

19. WINSTON'S TALE

Winston Churchill's elderly car cleared security and drove through the wrought-iron gates. He'd heard plenty about the place from his aide, and had been sent many of their decoded messages, but never been there in person. This wasn't a fact-finding mission like some he went on, to spot gaps in arrangements which smug locals had missed. The main point in this case was simply to tell the workers at the Park how much they were appreciated.

Although he deplored and downplayed the effect, most places he visited in war-torn Britain made some effort to welcome him. But he was more aware than any of his staff just how vital a job Bletchley Park was doing; and he didn't want to disrupt it, even for a morning. Moreover, he was aware that his own visits anywhere created a security risk: coming here had to be without fanfare or publicity. So this was not a well-trumpeted visit. He had decided to make the journey only the day before. The Park had had no chance to prepare for him – though he was unsure whether or not they would have done so. He'd never come across a more task-focused bunch of staff in all his life.

'Welcome aboard, sir,' said Sir Edward Travis, saluting, as the Prime Minister entered the panelled control room in the Bletchley Mansion. 'Is your aim today to see the key steps in the process, to meet our key people or to address the staff? And, to help us plan, how long will you be with us?'

'Hmm, I'll try to do all three, if I can, Sir Edward. But I'm only here for a couple of hours. I don't want to get in your way.'

Travis gave silent thanks for a top man who recognised areas where he was not an expert; and had the humility to admit the fact rather than to bluster on. He encouraged Churchill to continue.

'I'll never understand what you all do, Sir Edward. My skills are in words, not mathematics. I don't need to know anyway. What I want from you, first of all, is an honest assessment of anything I can do to help. Right now this is the most vital activity going on in this country. You've got our best brains here – is there anything more needed, to make them effective? Are you getting the enemy signals back fast enough? And, once you've decrypted them, are there any delays in getting the decoded messages back out? And most important of all, are we doing enough to keep the source of the messages hidden?'

Not many commanding officers in wartime Britain would hear that fulsome a message from the Prime Minister. Travis was astute enough not to waste the opportunity.

'Sir, our top mathematician, Alan Turing, has recently come up with a design for a radical calculating machine that could automate the search for the new keys – the starting positions for the Enigma wheels. The enemy change these every day at midnight. So the task of identifying the new positions is core to everything we do – and speed is essential. Turing's calculating machine will need specialist staff from the Post Office to build it: that could take several months.'

'OK. It's so mad it might even work. The whole damn thing sounds completely impossible. If someone here can see a way through we've got to give it our best shot. But if it changes every day how on earth do you cope?'

'Our enemy is methodically ruthless, sir – and ruthlessly methodical. As soon as we get a few messages from, say, the German army, we look for any sets of letters that they have in common. That'll probably be "Heil Hitler". Or if it's a weather forecast, it'll start "Here is the forecast". After that it's trial and error. But the great thing is that, once we've found the Enigma starting position for the day, we can apply it to message after message.'

Churchill asked more questions until he understood what was required to build the advanced calculator and then gave the scheme his complete approval. Next he moved on to the second aspect of his visit.

'What I'd like to do is to meet a few junior staff and hear from them, one by one, what they do. I won't remember much, mind. But you never know what might emerge. And I hope it'll give them and their colleagues a boost to know I'm interested in them.'

'Right, sir. That's an excellent thought. I'll get some coffee sent in. Plus a selection of staff – half a dozen, maybe – from different sides of the work here that you can have individual chats to.'

'Good. Make sure there's plenty of brandy, though, with the coffee.'

Although the date of Churchill's visit was secret, its possibility had been anticipated. Sir Edward Travis had not been told what would be required; but Churchill, too, was methodical in his way, so he had some clues. Each Bletchley Section Head had been asked to identify an articulate staff member and prime them for a chat with the war-time leader. Half a dozen phone calls later they were all called to the Mansion.

Molly Filbert was surprised to be among the group. She had felt she was in disgrace after becoming too close a friend with the man who'd left at short notice - destination, it was said, Southern Ireland. But her boss had been warned by the Security Chief of the need to restore her morale; he thought this was a way he could do so.

'So, Miss Filbert, what's your role here?' asked Churchill, once the girl had introduced herself. He liked girls with spirit.

'I'm a courier, sir. Once a week I go on a motor bike up to the North of Scotland to fetch the parcels. I start back just after midnight; I'm back by mid-morning. There's a team of us, we each cover one night a week.'

'Scotland, eh. I was an MP up there once, you know – it was a long time ago.' Churchill mused for a moment. 'What happens in winter – some of their storms are pretty fierce?'

'We get wet to the bone, sir – and even colder than usual. When the roads are completely blocked with snow we don't get sent. Once the forecast went wrong, there was an unexpected blizzard and I had to battle back through snowdrifts. It took me two days. But whatever happens I know the parcels are crucial to the work here.'

'That's true, my dear. It's a vital job that you all do.' Churchill leaned forward confidentially. 'Tell me, d'you know what the core of the work here actually is?'

'I don't sir. It's very intense and very important, though. And very secret.'

'Ah, yes, tell me: how do they enforce the security in a place like this?'

'You need a pass to get onto the base – even the gardeners have those. I was lodged with one until two months ago - he never got inside a building. Then you need a special pass for each hut. Those are checked each time at the hut door. If you've forgotten it, even if they know you, they won't let you in.'

'Good, good. So the enemy has no idea at all of what's going on.'

The girl looked downcast. 'We hope not, sir.'

Churchill pricked up his ears; he detected something amiss. He considered her words for a moment. 'You said . . . you said you used to lodge with a gardener. Did something happen? Why is he no longer here?'

Molly had feared, when she'd been chosen, that this might come to light. But she had been told by her boss to hold nothing back. 'The gardener – he was called Eamonn - left suddenly in the

117

dead of night. He caught a train to Liverpool. The security people told me he'd probably gone to Southern Ireland. But he was very shy. I was the only person her really talked to. And I was sure he'd got no documents or anything. It all happened a couple of months ago.'

Churchill asked her nothing more. But he made a note to raise the matter with Sir Edward Travis before he left.

An hour later the informal interviews were over. 'I'd like to finish off here with a short talk to your staff over lunch,' the Prime Minister told Sir Edward. 'I won't give any details away, but I want to reassure them their work is vital. And reinforce the need for security.'

'That would be excellent, sir. It's a fine day. Maybe you could talk to them on the lawn outside?'

'There might be one more thing I could help with. It's something you didn't mention earlier,' Churchill went on.

Travis looked puzzled. 'What's that, sir?'

'I'm sure that you have security in the Park under tight control. None of the people I talked to had a glimmering of the wider picture of what goes on here. And our Forces do their very best to hide the fact that we've got access to Enigma from the enemy. Sending up planes which "happen" to be over places where the enemy troops are known to be and so on. Even so, that may not be enough. One spy who drew special attention to this place could be enough to prompt a precautionary bombing raid. Which might be enough to seriously damage the base – or, worse still, the key boffins.'

'My staff and I have been round this time and again, sir. What else could we do?'

Churchill leaned forward, looking almost conspiratorial. 'Disinformation, Sir Edward.'

Travis looked bemused. 'Could you elaborate, sir?'

118

'Your team here is the hub of what we do – I use your results every day. But there is another part of our security apparatus that is more, shall we say, disreputable. Their role is not to find out what the enemy are saying or doing but rather to plant information which is, shall we say, subtly unhelpful.'

Now Sir Edward saw where his distinguished visitor was heading. 'You mean double agents?'

'Precisely. Even I don't know how it's done but I guess there must be German agents we've uncovered who we've left in place, so they can be used to pass on such "information". Suppose that we sent out information through one of these double agents . . .'

'About a bogus Bletchley. Well away from here.'

' We could let slip that we had a special camp linked to decoding based, say, around Manchester. That's out of reach of their bombers. We've plenty of bases like this one, scattered all over the country, doing all sorts of administration. There's bound to be one near Manchester. We could toughen it up a bit, add some aerials, send in big cars every so often – maybe even arrange for staff to do courier trips around the country.'

'You mean, sir, we could create an alternative site, that might possibly be doing what we're doing?'

'Precisely. Or even several. If different agents identified a series of sites, at random intervals from now on, we'd confuse the enemy. Our best hope is that no precise message about Bletchley Park and its activities will ever get through. But if it does, we can at least make sure it's not received in splendid isolation.'

119

Still on display at Bletchley Park, the world's first computer. This was designed by Alan Turing to grind through millions of possible starting positions for the day used on all the enemy Enigma machines.

20. SUNSET BOULEVARD

'My suggestion is a bowl of flour and treacle over the kitchen door,' said Matilda, 'put there just when she's about to show round some new guests.'

'Trouble is, it might miss her, but hit the guests,' mused Grace. 'I'd prefer to target the garden hose, then turn it on just when she's getting into her car.'

The more alert residents of the Sunset Old Peoples Care Home were playing their usual afternoon parlour game of "Zap the Matron". Martha, the Home's Matron, seemed to despise them with a passion; there had arisen in response a common hatred of her, which was played out in these fantasies.

Albert, one of the livelier inmates, had suffered a particular bout of scorn only the day before. He had been pushing Wilhelmina gently down the garden path when he had been accosted by a bee. In the resulting confusion Albert had let go of the wheelchair. It had careered at increasing speed down the garden, finally overturning into the blackcurrant bushes at the bottom.

It was bad luck that these bushes were out of sight; also that Albert had been so afflicted by the pain of his bee sting that, by the time he'd applied medication, he'd quite forgotten about the old lady.

It was a hot day and most of the residents were sheltering indoors. Wilhelmina's absence had not been noted until supper time. She was quite sprightly – for 93 – but not agile enough to extract herself from a position of being head-first in the bushes.

121

Once she was rescued she was quite upset — not with Albert, of course, but with Martha, for failing to search for her earlier.

Martha had one day off each week. No-one knew how she spent it. Cover was provided by staff from the "Care to the Dismal End" agency, most of whom spent the day in the Home's office, catching up on their reading. The next such day came just after Wilhelmina's fall - and Albert's fall from grace.

When the residents met for their afternoon Zap, Albert was still hurting. 'We shouldn't just treat this as a game. We should really make her suffer.'

The other Zap players were eager to respond. 'She drinks plenty — and all her wine bottles are in the cellar,' observed Matilda. 'They'll all be screw cap these days. Why don't we dilute them with vinegar?' It seemed a fair response.

The cellar was out of bounds, but the agency carer wasn't watching; and the door wasn't locked, only bolted. With Matilda on guard, it didn't take Albert long to creep down into the cellar. He returned a few minutes later, six bottles of vintage red wine in his shopping bag.   Great glee was had by the residents in drinking some of the wine before adding the replacement vinegar.

'Those steps are very steep,' reported Albert, when he returned, tottering slightly, from taking back the modified bottles, 'and there's no natural light in that cellar. It's a pity we can't trap her down there for a day or two.'

'Well, she goes down to fetch a fresh bottle of wine most evenings,' noted Grace. 'At least she wouldn't die of thirst.'

So, gradually, the plan was hatched.

It was a week later when Martha made the fateful trip into the cellar. The Zap players were watching and knew this was the critical day. As she disappeared, Albert crept over to the cupboard under the stairs and opened the fuse box. Then he flipped the fuse switch that he had found, from earlier experiment, controlled the only light in the cellar.

Meanwhile Matilda slipped over to the cellar door, closed it and rammed the bolts closed. A muffled cry of annoyance and alarm came up from the depths. It was followed by a solid thud as Martha tripped over the bottom step in the pitch dark, banged her head on the cellar wall and collapsed onto the floor.

The residents who had been in on the scheme noted the silence with some relief; their plan had not extended beyond this point anyway. The rest of the Home's guests had long lost the capacity to note anything much at all.

The next day the agency relief staff turned up. She was surprised that Martha was not there for a handover, but not concerned enough to take remedial action.

But by the day after the zappers felt some qualms. The fuse had been restored and the bolts undone, but there was no sign of Martha emerging. The relief agency was called, the problem of the missing Matron explained and a search conducted. It did not take long to discover Martha's body in the cellar, alongside many smashed bottles of wine. The alcoholic haze seemed to blend in with her condition.

The arrival of the police a few hours later was unexpected but perhaps inevitable. Inspector Hughes rounded up the residents and ushered them into the lounge, where he could explain the situation. Noting that many of the old dears had hearing aids, he realised that he would need to shout.

'I'm sorry to have to tell you all,' he bellowed, 'that your Matron, Martha, was found dead in the cellar here earlier today. At first sight it looks like the result of a dreadful accident. It appears that she fell over the bottom step, banged her head on the corner of the wall, collapsed and later died.'

There were noises of shock from the residents. One old dear was heard explaining to her even deafer neighbour that Martha had been hurt while banging her head into her bottom. 'I'm not surprised. I never thought she was that double-jointed,' her neighbour replied.

Further along the row the elderly Wilhelmina fainted. The policeman had to divert his efforts into first aid until she was revived.

'My only problem,' the Inspector continued, feeling exhausted and wishing he'd thought to bring a loudhailer with him, 'is that this is not the first time something like this has happened. I gather from the Trustees that Martha is the second Matron to have died in this Home in the course of her duties.'

'But Sally didn't die in the cellar,' protested one old dear. 'She just didn't come back from a trip to collect some spare blankets from the attic. It was just a pity the attic door had jammed shut.'

'I'm sure she shouted for help,' added her friend, 'It wasn't true that we ignored her. It's just that most of us are a little deaf, so we didn't hear her.'

'And we told the agency staff she was missing, as soon as we saw them. That was only a week later,' concluded a third member of their little group. 'But by then, the ambulance man who they summoned told us, she had been substantially dehydrated.'

The residents didn't seem too upset by the memory. Inspector Hughes wasn't sure if he was being mocked subtly, or was simply confronting senility. But he wasn't sure that he could summon the energy to argue with his superiors for the resources he would need to conduct an in-depth investigation of an Old People's Home.

Whatever happened, whichever geriatric was arrested, there would be no good headlines in it for the police.

He drew a deep breath.

'Alright, I can't prove that anything deliberate happened to Martha either. But I'm just warning you all, that to lose two of your Matrons whilst on duty might seem accidental; but to lose any more will be seriously careless.'

Later that afternoon the more alert of the residents gathered for a meeting. They were not unduly disturbed by the departure of Martha; but they realised they would need to find a replacement to look after the Home. No-one had much confidence in the 'Dismal End' agency.

'Do you think the applicants will hear about what happened to Sally - and now to Martha?'

'They won't be afraid of a bunch of old fogeys like us – surely?'

'Probably not. But even so, it won't be easy to find someone. Young people don't trust us, you know.'

'Even the politicians are after us now,' said a gloomy resident who had watched the latest budget.

'The trouble is,' said Wilhelmina, who was seated on the edge of the circle, 'that I've only got one more possible granddaughter.'

There was silence as the rest of the group tried to make sense of this comment.

'Sorry,' said Albert, eventually, 'I'm not sure I understand. Are you telling us that Sally and Martha were both relatives of yours? Is that why they came here?'

'My family believe that I'm extremely wealthy,' said Wilhelmina. 'So for years they've all looked for opportunities to make sure I remember them in my will. That's why it was easy for me to attract Sally to work here; and after her Martha. But neither of them was very caring to any of us, were they?'

'My only other granddaughter is called Janice. She's due out of Holloway Prison any day now. Shall I send her an invitation?'

21. GRIEF FINDS AN OUTLET

'Here are the recent figures, Job,' said Thomas Staveley, 'and look: there are the dips. Any ideas?'

Pulling at his long beard, the avuncular Job Hockaday studied the weekly record. He saw that, once every few weeks, the contributions had fallen alarmingly. 'Who was taking those particular offerings?'

The collection at Delabole Chapel was usually taken by the young people. This was why the bespectacled, pernickety Treasurer had approached Hockaday, the Sunday School Superintendant.

Subsequent investigation revealed that Bessie Cowling was always the one on duty when the collection dipped. 'Hm,' said Hockaday, 'I'd better have a word.'

'How are you coping, my dear?' Hockaday asked Bessie, a few days later. 'You seem so sad these days.' Though he didn't spell it out, both of them knew it was less than two years since the Delabole Slate Quarry Disaster of 1869. More than a dozen had died and ten-year old Bessie, innocently taking afternoon tea to her dad as he worked on the steep incline, had nearly been one of them.

As one of those who'd narrowly escaped on that dreadful day, Hockaday wondered, could she be suffering long-term after-effects? The girl looked dishevelled and untidy, ink smudges on her left hand. He remembered, sadly, how she used to look so presentable.

'I'm alright in myself, sir. It's my best friend Fannie that I miss.'

126

Bessie sniffed. 'Despite all their efforts, they've still not found her body under all those thousands of tons of rubble. It was my fault she was on them cliffs. Her friends have never really forgiven me.'

Hockaday reached out his arm to comfort her. 'I'm sure that's not true, Bessie. The whole community's been affected, in so many different ways: it's just that grief takes many forms. A dozen families have lost their bread-winner. We've all got to keep going: not to let our standards slip. Don't worry, my dear, we'll have a memorial service for your beloved Fannie one day.'

He sensed her tears were not far away – to be honest, he was feeling pretty wretched himself. In the circumstances Hockaday was reluctant to push any harder; but he resolved to watch carefully when Bessie was next on duty.

Two weeks later Bessie's turn came round and Hockaday laid his plans. Immediately before the service he called her over. 'Bessie, I had to leave my daughter at home, feeling sick.'

'I'll go and sit with her if you like, Mr Hockaday.'

Bessie seemed happy enough to abandon her collecting duty – surely a good sign? Hockaday asked another youngster to cover for her then sat back to see what would happen.

Delabole Chapel was a grey, austere building, with aisles down both sides and pews in the middle. At the back of the main hall an upper gallery had been added, with stairs on either side, normally claimed by the younger generation. It was the stairs, of course, which made young folk the chapel's preferred collection takers.

What would happen today if Bessie was missing? Despite the Treasurer's statistics, Hockaday found it hard to believe this reliable girl would rob the collection: he'd known her family for years. But if not, was someone out to blacken her name; and if so, who - and why?

He watched the offering carefully but could see nothing amiss.

'There's nothing odd in the offerings this week,' said Staveley afterwards. So perhaps Bessie was the guilty party: but there was still no direct evidence.

Six weeks went by and then Bessie was on duty again. This time Hockaday let her take the collection. But he also arranged for a steward to be seated at the back of the building so he could see any adjustment Bessie made to the bag, on its way up to the gallery.

At the end of the service he waited with bated breath for the Treasurer's verdict.

'The offering's right down again, I'm afraid,' reported Staveley. 'Look, Job, we can't keep it secret. The congregation has to be told. After all, it's their money that's disappearing.'

'If you do that, Thomas, we might stem the problem but we won't solve it: and we'll never be sure who and why. Later on it might start all over again.'

'But the Chapel will no longer be robbed, Job. It's not just a token offering: we need that money, to fix the roof and pay the Minister.'

'At the end of the day people matter more than money, Thomas. Please, give me one more chance to work out what's happening. We have to know if Bessie is the thief or the victim.'

On weekdays Job Hockaday was the Commercial Manager at the Slate Quarry. He asked himself how he would tackle the problem if it arose there; then transferred his thinking over to the Chapel.

Soon Bessie was on duty again. Anticipating this, Hockaday quietly slipped a signed note into the collection bag beforehand then waited to see what would happen. The offering was taken as usual. At the end of the service he crept to the back room as the Treasurer counted the cash given.

'It's not good, Job,' he said. 'The amount's right down again.'

Hockaday did not answer directly. Instead he picked up the collection bag and gave it a shake. Nothing fell out: his signature slip

128

had disappeared.

'The thing is, Thomas, this bag wasn't the one Bessie started with. It must have been swapped at some point – almost certainly as the collection was being taken.'

Staveley was staggered. 'That's systematic fraud, Job - even worse than we thought. It can't go on. We've got to make an announcement.'

'Just one more trial, Thomas – I beg you. If that doesn't solve it, I agree, we'll tell the whole church.'

'Hm, what are you going to do?'

'Well, we know when it'll happen again. This time we need to make sure the bag can't be swapped without us knowing. I'll pin a piece of yellow card to the outside. Then we'll both watch it like hawks as the collection's taken. Try and see exactly when the switchover occurs.'

Six weeks later the plan was put into effect. Hockaday had experimented beforehand to find the size of card needed, to be seen down the length of the Chapel. As the service began he pinned the card to the bag.

Treasurer and Superintendant, along with other chapel leaders, had seats at the front, facing the congregation; they could watch unobtrusively as the service progressed. Eventually the point was reached where the offertory hymn was announced.

Exchanging glances, Job and Thomas prepared to monitor the bag as Bessie started down the aisle, handing it to the man on the end of the row then moving back to collect it when it was passed back along the row behind. The yellow card was still there; and it remained in view as Bessie tackled row after row.

Finally, she reached the rear row and started to climb the stairs. Was this where the swap occurred?

The side of the Chapel where Bessie had disappeared was bathed in bright sunshine. Hockaday breathed a sigh of relief, a moment later, as Bessie appeared upstairs: he could see the yellow card was still in place. The girl stepped down to the front row and handed over the bag, ready to be passed along. This row was occupied by youngsters, most of whom, it seemed, felt no need to contribute to the Chapel's finances. It didn't take it long to reach the far end.

But as the bag was passed, in the comparative gloom, to the row behind, Hockaday sensed rather than saw a sleight of hand; then a bag without a yellow tag started its journey back towards Bessie.

The hymn being sung was one of Charles Wesley's longest. The eighteenth century had no need of sound-bites. Seven verses in, there were still three to go.

Without a word Hockaday slipped quietly from his seat, down the aisle, up the matching set of stairs to those used by Bessie and then down to the front row. By the time he'd been spotted by the youngsters it was too late. The collection bag, with its tell-tale yellow marker, was still visible, half-hidden beneath the seat, as its twin made its way back to Bessie.

'We'll talk about this later,' Hockaday whispered to the startled youngsters, as he grabbed the original bag. At last he knew who was responsible.

Later the three lads involved made their way to the Treasurer's office. They had been caught red-handed: there was no point in claiming total innocence. 'Sir, we weren't stealing the collection - just putting it to a better use.'

Staveley looked like he was about to explode. Hockaday, though, had learned to gather the whole story before dispensing justice. Solemnly he invited them to continue.

'Every few weeks, sir, we've been adding it to Fannie's Memorial Fund. When her body is found we want it to be a really special memorial.'

It was clear Bessie was not the only one grieving the lost girl.

The nine-year old Fannie was a loss to them all. That was some sort of explanation; but still not the whole story.

'So why did you only try this when Bessie was in charge?' Hockaday asked. 'Were you trying to make sure she would be the one to take the blame if it all went wrong?'

The lads looked stunned. 'It was nothing like that, sir.'

'So what was it?'

The oldest lad took the lead. 'Every other collector comes up on the darker side of the Chapel. Bessie came up the sunny side and left us in the gloom. She didn't know it - but she was the only one who gave us a chance to build up our late friend's Memorial Fund.'

'I'm afraid I still don't understand, said Hockaday, frowning.

'It's easy, sir. Bessie's the only one on the collection rota, see, who's left-handed.'

*The Slate Quarry at Delabole. The cliff collapse which preceded this story took place in 1869. It's also the starting-point for the drama behind the second Cornish Conundrum, **"Slate Expectations"**.*

22. GUMDROP STRIKES AGAIN

The key had been found, but what to do with it? Nicholas retrieved the battered object from the plant pot at the rear of the ramshackle outhouse then turned to make his escape. It would be stupid to be caught at this late stage. He was almost sure it was the right key, how could he be certain? His reputation, as the outfit's appointed fixer, hung by a thread.

He found his fellow-conspirator, Patrick, lurking outside. 'I've got it,' he whispered, 'the gardener was correct. He told me the first thing Jeremy did on arrival was to go round the back.'

'Hm, let's see if it does the trick.'

Patrick took the key and led the way to the front of the house. There, gleaming in the early-morning sun, was a vintage, olive-green, open-top Bentley. The key wasn't needed to get in – neither door had a lock, and in any case could easily be climbed over. But one was needed to release the engine. Patrick inserted it – and gave a cry of joy as the key turned.

'They didn't have starter motors in 1930,' said Nicholas. 'I'll have to use the starting handle. Make sure it's out of gear, will you? I'd rather not be run over before we're even out of the drive.'

He strode round to the front and seized the starting handle. He'd never done this before: which way did it turn? He guessed clockwise and gave a big heave. But nothing happened.

After two more tries he walked back to peer over Patrick's shoulder at the dashboard. 'All these old cars had chokes. Can you see one?'

'What am I looking for? The only choke I've ever come across

132

was on my lawn mower.'

Leaning over, Nicholas spotted a knob below the steering-wheel. 'Try pulling that.'

Swiftly – for time was precious – he returned to the front of the car, seized the starting handle once more and gave another heave. This time there were signs of life; and after one more go, with some hesitation, the engine started to rumble its way into life.

Nicholas moved round to the passenger side and climbed aboard. Relief - now they could be on their way.

Slowly, Patrick drove the car out onto the country road. At five in the morning there was no-one about. The vintage Bentley couldn't go fast, but fortunately they didn't have far to go.

They drove steadily through Much Wittering, past the Dalmatian, where the observant gardener had been so helpful the night before, and out the other side. Two miles further on they came to the production village, with its phalanx of tents and equipment, including two more vintage vehicles. A small crowd, dressed in inter-war clothing, was milling about; a cheer greeted their arrival.

'It's Nick who's saved the day,' explained Patrick, once they'd pulled in. 'He remembered his Uncle Jeremy had a vintage car. He was away, so it was just a matter of finding the key.'

'I'm sure he wouldn't mind me borrowing it if he was around,' added Nicholas. 'And we'll take care to put it back exactly where we found it.'

The filming of "Gumdrop foils the Gang" had been under way for several weeks. Most of the required scenes were now captured. There was just the final car-chase left to film. That would have been straightforward if the second car hadn't broken down a couple of days ago. The mechanic had declared it needed a new clutch and gearbox – not the easiest items to find in a hurry for a 1928 Bentley.

A day of panic had ensued. Was the film to be wrecked, at the last moment, by mechanical failure?

Nicholas was employed by the film company as all-round fixer. This was certainly a fixing challenge. He had spent most of the day on the phone, but to no avail. Given a fortnight, the problem could easily be solved; but the leading members of the cast were on fixed-term contracts and had other work to go on to. It had been in the evening, when the company had retired to drown their sorrows in the Dalmatian, that he remembered he had been to this pub before with his Uncle; and then – with excitement - that the old man used to own a vintage Bentley.

For once the sun was shining; there was no time to lose. Swiftly the film producer, Patrick, ordered the various camera crews to their pre-determined positions along the chosen route. The cast were settled in their respective cars. Gumdrop – a blue Austin Clifton Heavy 12/4, just as in the original stories - was prepared for the chase.

'I want to shoot this chase scene just the once,' said Patrick, as he sat in his Range Rover ready to follow, with Nicholas beside him. 'We'll do the final fight scene in close-up, separately, once Gumdrop's driver has cornered the pair in the Bentley, down in the woods. Give it your best shot, everyone. Let's go.'

It was only a performance but there was excitement in the air. The two men playing the villains had the harder job, of course; they'd no previous experience of the borrowed Bentley. But there was no time to practise; Patrick reckoned that a cavalier and haphazard road-style would add to the film's watchability.

It was early morning in remote Dorset: no other cars about. The villains' Bentley started down the road, with Gumdrop a few hundred yards behind. Neither car was fast by modern standards, but with open tops and noisy engines they seemed fast enough.

The road reached the top of the hill. This was the point at which, on the production's safety plan, speeds should have dropped. But the Bentley's driver was caught up in the excitement of the chase. Faster and faster he went down the slope. All was fine until the car reached the bend at the start of the wood.

Even then the villains might have got away with it if they had not met the car coming the other way. It was the old village taxi, on its way back from the nearby station. Both cars jammed on their brakes and skidded into their respective hedges. They came to a halt side by side, inches apart, both with wheels in the road-side mud.

Gumdrop came on them a few seconds later and its driver – the film's hero - jammed on his brakes. It was touch and go; then he too came to a halt, inches behind the Bentley.

Finally Patrick and Nicholas joined the melée, braking sharply behind the rest.

The actors knew this scene was being filmed as a one-off. Swiftly the villains jumped out of the Bentley and into the woods; Gumdrop's driver followed close behind. There were the sounds of a robust fight breaking out.

Nicholas, though, had lost interest in the film. He had seen who was sitting in the taxi: it was his Uncle Jeremy.

He gulped. His Uncle could scarcely fail to notice his distinctive Bentley, squashed in the road alongside him.

But his Uncle was not as upset as he feared. 'That's my car?'

'Yes, Uncle. You see –'

'But - how did you find the key? I put it somewhere and couldn't remember where. I haven't been able to use the car for weeks.'

It would be a long story. But, miraculously, it would end well.

Nicholas, was, after all, a fixer.

A vintage car in Mousehole. In the narrow streets being thin has its advantages.

23. STANLEY ENCOUNTERS LIVINGSTONE

Yoda Kugari completed her circuit of the Savuti vegetable market, added some interesting spices and a bundle of tomatoes to her shoulder bag then turned to catch the matatu back to her village. The crowded minibuses didn't operate to any known timetable but she knew – by some mystic process of osmosis – that there was one now about to leave.

She was surprised, as she waited, to see a middle-aged white man wander down the street and head for the Post Office. There weren't many "Europeans" (as all whites were labelled) in this remote part of north Botswana. If he stayed around for any length of time he might be company for her employer.

Yoda had never travelled far from home – she'd never been outside Botswana. Her formal education was limited to reading, writing and speaking an African form of English; but she was intrinsically bright. She had an instinct about how things worked, who was in charge and how they could best be bypassed. Under the guidance of Irwin – her boss - she had even learned to play chess. They played most evenings and she could occasionally beat him. Of course, she had no way of knowing if that meant she was a genius or Irwin was a duffer. He was certainly a man shy of company. Most of his time was spent in his study, working away on his latest book.

In a white man's world that would be a sign of intelligence but here in Africa the world of books was obscure and misunderstood.

'I'm back, Massa,' she announced an hour later as she reached the compound containing the faded, small, ex-colonial bungalow and the mud-hut behind which was her home. 'Some news: I saw a white man in Savuti. You know him?'

Irwin sighed. 'You credit me with too much wisdom, Yoda. There are a billion white men in the world, millions just in Africa. I can't possibly know them all. Did you happen to catch his name?'

'No, Massa. I called him Scrawny. But he was wearing new-looking shorts and sun hat and he went into the Post Office. So he was probably a newcomer to Africa, looking for someone. It might have been you. He was about your age.'

Irwin did not rate her observation on age. Not many Batswanas lived beyond the age of fifty and to Yoda all white men who'd reached forty probably looked much the same.

Even so he sounded old for a Peace Corps. They normally wandered round in twos and threes. And if he was a soldier he would certainly be in uniform. The United Nations peacekeepers who occasionally passed through the area knew that it was easier to demand the best provisions and accommodation under the pressure of arms.

It said quite a lot about the shallowness of his life in Botswana that the unknown stranger had taken even this much of his attention. But an unknown European was potentially a threat. It would be good to learn more about him if he stayed around for long – but for evasive purposes only.

Yoda had a more upbeat view of the stranger's potential. Tribal bonds lay deep in her psyche. In the market, say, she felt most comfortable with fellow Baleyans from Livingstone, even if she'd never previously met them. Her extended family knew few bounds. And if she could find Irwin a friend – another white, a fellow European – he would surely be less grumpy. He might even be less inclined to strike her when drunk. That didn't happen often but she would rather it didn't happen at all.

Two days later, on her regular pattern, Yoda returned to Savuti market. She had her usual household purchases to make – it didn't pay to carry stocks far ahead. But she also had another target in mind.

Irwin would not have a clue on tracking down a white man in Savuti but for Yoda it was a doddle. If Scrawny was in town she would find him. There were only a limited number of bars where the Europeans would congregate; the most popular was one with what they called a "television". If Scrawny had been in any of them in the past few days, one of the Baleyans who worked there would have seen him – and would tell her where he'd gone. It was absurdly simple.

Yoda had not meant to do more, today, than find out Scrawny's proper name – that seemed to be all Irwin could relate to. But when she found him drinking alone, in the second bar she tried, 'Satan's Shadow', it seemed too good an opportunity to miss.

As always, there was a Baleyan behind the bar. Speaking in their common language, he told Yoda that "Scrawny" had been there for some time and could be there for a while longer: he'd booked one of the guest rooms upstairs for a fortnight. His name – or at least the one he'd registered under - was "Jack Stanley". She ordered a bottle of coca cola and wandered over towards her target.

Jack had been wondering how he could take his search forward. The damp heat was oppressive, the pace of life was tortoise-like and he was working entirely alone. There were some positives: the locals in Savuti seemed friendly enough. He didn't feel under any threat here, though he hadn't risked going out in the evenings. They understood his English after a fashion, though they mostly spoke in their local language – or languages, he had no idea how many. But he had no clue on how to take his quest any further.

That was, until the local woman stopped at his table and greeted him. 'Mr Stanley, how are you?'

'I am fine,' he smiled, following the form of words he had ob-

139

served. 'I'm sorry, should I know you?'

For a moment he wondered if he was about to be propositioned. But it was the middle of the day. The woman looked respectable enough, with her long green robe, braided hair and dark eyes; and she moved with a serene grace.

He was forgetting his manners. 'Please - would you like to sit down?'

Without haste she took a chair. 'My name is Yoda. No, I don't think we have met before. I've lived around here all my life.'

'Yoda.' He nodded: he could get his tongue round that. 'And mine is Jack – Jack Stanley. I'm from England.'

'Mr Stanley.' She looked at him. 'I work for a man from England. Do you know him?'

'I suppose I might,' said Stanley cautiously. 'But I've not been here long. What's his name?'

'I call him Mr Irwin. His full name, he told me once, is Irwin Livingstone. Like the town, he explained.'

Stanley frowned and then his face lit up. 'Yes, there is a town of that name around here. But the town is named after an explorer - David Livingstone. He came here a long time ago.'

'Maybe . . . maybe my boss is from the same tribe?' hazarded Yoda. She could see that Stanley didn't latch on to the name.

'What else can you tell me about him, Yoda?'

'Mr Irwin doesn't come out very often. Most of the time he just sits in his study, writing books.'

Two words which might be nothing - or might be everything. Jack knew that Henry Grimthorpe had belonged to a Writers' Circle before he disappeared. He had no other lead to follow, anyway.

'I'm here for a few days, Yoda. Do you think it would be possible to meet him? I'm interested in books too – or, at least, in meeting their authors.'

Irwin Livingstone was livid when Yoda got back and told him her news. For a second she feared he was going to beat her. She pressed on with her findings.

'He says his name is Jack Stanley. So now do you know him?'

'I once knew someone called Jack – though only briefly. In Tamworth. I never found out his second name. He was a very wicked man, Yoda: he went to prison for murdering his wife. I hope it's not the same person.'

'The man I met didn't seem very wicked, Mr Irwin. He just wanted to meet a famous author. I told him you were too shy to come into town so I agreed I'd bring him out here the day after tomorrow.'

Yoda could see that Irwin was rattled though she had little idea why. Two men from the same tribe should surely have plenty in common?

Yoda had given herself the intervening day before the two men met for a reason. It gave her time to meet once more with Mr Jack at Satan's Shadow and project back her boss's anxieties.

'Mr Jack, where you come from in England?' she asked.

'I doubt you've had heard of it. It's a place called Tamworth.'

It might be obscure but he could see from the look on her face that the name meant something. Jack swallowed hard. 'Is that . . . is that where Irwin comes from?'

Yoda was in confusion. That was the trouble with these Europeans - you never knew which of them was telling the truth. Africans never told the whole truth, of course, but she always knew who was lying. She could see nothing for it but to explain further.

'Mr Irwin, he told me that he once knew a man called Jack in Tamworth but he landed in prison for murder. Was . . . was that you, sir?'

Jack's face had blackened. 'Eight and a half years and the swine is still lying. Yoda, I'm very sorry, but your boss was lying to you.' He sighed. 'Yes, it's true, I went to prison: but that was because

141

they got the wrong man. The man who did the murder was Irwin – or Henry as he called himself in those days, Henry Grimthorpe. That's why I've come out here to find him and settle the score.'

'But how did you know to come here?'

'I had a long time in prison to plan it out. I knew Henry would disappear and change his name – probably go abroad. I doubt he spoke any language other than English. But he wouldn't want to be anywhere where justice was too demanding. Back of beyond in Africa would suit him fine.'

Botswana didn't seem back of beyond to Yoda but she let that go. 'Africa's a big place, Mr Jack.'

'I didn't know much about him – we only met a few times. Then I remembered him mentioning a Writers' Circle. I had plenty of time in prison so I wrote to all the ones based around Tamworth till I found it. They told me that Henry Grimthorpe used to belong but he had moved away.'

'I'm sorry, I don't understand. How did that help?'

'I was in prison. I couldn't attend in person but I registered an interest from Australia. My sister emigrated there; she'd send me the occasional poem. I'd hack it about then send it in as my own. And I kept track of the Circle's membership list as it updated over the years.'

Yoda had never heard of a Writers' Circle, didn't understand the details, but she could see roughly where he was heading. 'And did they get another overseas member?'

Gee, she was bright. 'That's right. The name wasn't Grimthorpe anymore but the address was Savuti in northern Botswana, close to the Zambian border - the sort of place a runaway Englishman might head. I got a ticket to the Botswana capital - Gaborone - as soon as they let me out. It was a gamble but I'd got nowhere else to go.' He shook his head. 'There was no-one left at home.'

If he was telling her the truth, Yoda, thought, it was a very sad tale. But was he – and was it the whole truth?

Later that morning she found an internet cafe and, with a little help, accessed Google. What could she find about a murder in Tamworth eight or nine years ago? That was in the internet era and she found it had good newspaper coverage. She read it all very carefully indeed.

Next day, Jack Stanley had refused to travel to Irwin Livingstone's compound in a crowded matatu and insisted that Yoda send him a taxi.

It didn't make much difference, Yoda, thought: the problem wasn't the vehicle as much as the state of the road. 'Are your roads car-worthy?' had been a recent election slogan but it hadn't led to better roads. Jack didn't realise just how far they had to travel: Irwin had chosen to live right in the back of the back of beyond. Yoda was now starting to understand why.

Both protagonists had thought hard about the forthcoming meeting and how it would be conducted. Irwin's first thought had been to deny his existence; but if Jack could find him here (he had no idea how) he could probably find him anywhere. It was better to confront than to hide. Jack, for his part, had waited a long time and come a long way; he was not going anywhere. But he might as well start off by being civil.

Yoda had been asked 'to prepare a special banquet, as English as you can make it' and had spent hours slaving over her charcoal stove. Her role today was to act as waitress – and perhaps as referee.

'Jack, it's good to see you again,' began Irwin, offering his hand.

Reluctantly Jack responded. His body was still recovering from two hours of rough shaking in the taxi; he suspected the driver had taken the longest possible route – maybe Yoda had prompted him to do so.

'You took a bit of tracking down,' he replied. 'What should I call you nowadays – Henry or Irwin?'

143

His host was not fazed. 'Everyone in Africa has two names. Irwin is my day-name; in the local language it means "Thursday born". It'd probably be less confusing for Yoda if you stuck to that. By the way, you seem to have lost weight since we last met.'

'It's odd you should mention that, Irwin. It's one of the side effects of prison. There's not much exercise - but then there's not much food either. You should try it sometime.'

'Dear, dear. I hardly think prison would suit me at all. So what went wrong? The last time we met you'd got a perfectly decent alibi to cover the death of Maria – and I smothered her very gently. Did you forget your lines or something?'

'There were questions about Maria, Irwin, but no more than suspicions. My problem was that I'd claimed, when the police arrived, to be Henry Grimthorpe – as you and I had agreed. I'd got all his papers in the jacket you left me. And once you've given a name to the police, I found, it's very hard to casually change it.'

'So why was that a problem?'

'Because, Irwin, the police went on to discover a second body, under the kitchen floor.'

Irwin looked shocked and Jack continued. 'Of course I denied everything. Unfortunately, as I'm sure you know, the dead woman was my partner. And touchingly, she had my picture in the locket around her neck. So even though I denied everything, everyone took me as guilty – including the twelve men of the jury. Fifteen years I got – which reduced to eight with good behaviour.'

Jack paused then continued. 'I behaved very well, Irwin, because I wanted to make sure I caught up with you. That's a lot of time you owe me.'

Yoda thought it was time to intervene. 'Gentlemen, would you like to eat as you talk? The meal is all ready. And what would you like to drink?'

There was a conversational silence while the men sat down and the food was brought in. Irwin had raided his stock of fine white wine which he'd obtained last year from South Africa. Jack smiled. Whatever his later intentions, he was still partial to a good drink after his many years in prison.

Irwin had used the intervening moments to ponder Jack's account. 'Seems to me, Jack, that our plan worked pretty well, as far as Maria was concerned. We arranged an alibi and it worked. But I'm mystified by the dead woman found under the kitchen floor – and it was your partner, you say? I'm utterly astounded. Nothing to do with me, I assure you. But, as I recall, you wanted to find her body – or at least a body that could be claimed as hers – so you could recover her life insurance. Did you manage to make any headway on that?'

Jack had started on the yam-topped shepherd's pie and realised how hungry his years in prison had made him. The gravy, boosted by local spices, looked delicious and he took a large helping. And there was nothing wrong with the South African wine either. He mused on what Irwin had just said.

'Let me get this straight, Irwin. You're telling me that, even though you murdered your own wife for our mutual gain, you weren't responsible for Gwen's death?'

'I never met your wife. I don't even know what she looked like.'

Whatever might be said of his previous assertions, this line sounded genuine. Had Jack spent the last eight years blaming the wrong man? Was his journey here all in vain? For the moment baffled, he gave himself another helping of yam shepherd's pie.

Yoda topped up his gravy and made sure Irwin had plenty as well. The first bottle of wine was already empty and Yoda opened a second.

'Well who the hell did kill her?' asked Jack. 'And how did she get into your kitchen - and under the floor?' It was a strong wine and his head was starting to spin.

'Maria and I had had the floor done, just before your troubles. I did most of the work myself. There was one night when I left a

145

layer of concrete just starting to set while I went to my Writers'
Circle. Suppose . . . suppose that your Gwen was a friend of my
Maria –'

'My Gwen had some sort of decorating business – she could
have done a job for Maria.'

'Maybe they were lovers? And then had a row -'

'In which my Gwen was killed.'

'So my Maria shoved your Gwen into the concrete. By morning
the concrete was set and I just carried on covering it with slate
tiles. Well. So, in a sense, my smothering Maria was a form of
natural justice for your Gwen.'

Both men had more shepherd's pie and gravy and Yoda topped
up their glasses. They were both finding it harder to make conversation. The fire had gone out of Jack and Irwin looked relieved but
tired.

'There's one thing I don't understand.'

They'd almost forgotten Yoda was still there. Goodness knows
what she made of this conversation. It was hard to concentrate but
he must try. With massive effort Irwin looked up. 'Yes, Yoda?'

'Well, if two men agree to commit a murder, are they not both
guilty - even if only one does the deed?'

'Technically, I suppose, that's true,' replied Irwin. Jack nodded
his agreement, though he could dimly sense that this was a dan-
gerous concession.

'So in that case you're both guilty of Maria's death, aren't you?'

Irwin felt immensely tired. 'I don't know what you put in that
shepherd's pie, Yoda, but it's made me very sleepy. I don't think I
can answer that right now.'

He slumped down. His companion had already fallen into a deep
sleep.

Looking at the two dying men, Yoda felt a deep sense of peace.
Natural justice had prevailed. Her fellow Baleyan had warned her
to use only miniscule portions of the special spices, "to help them

sleep", but she'd spooned in the lot. Mercifully the wine had hidden the taste. And the concoction had certainly worked.

The taxi man was due back later. He would take Jack's body back to Savuti and he'd be found next morning in his room at Satan's Shadow – cause of death "unknown".

As for Irwin . . . well, the taxi driver was used to burying bodies and there was plenty of space on the compound. All that she needed was to contrive a spurious exit for Irwin from Botswana. There must be some ideas on that in his unpublished material.

The town of Arua, in north-west Uganda. But it could be any small town in Africa. Tamale, Ghana, where I spent four years teaching in the early 1970s, looked much the same.

44859569R00089

Made in the USA
Charleston, SC
10 August 2015